CAN'T RUN

(A Nora Price Mystery—Book 1)

Kate Bold

Kate Bold

Bestselling author Kate Bold is author of the ALEXA CHASE SUSPENSE THRILLER series, comprising six books (and counting); the ASHLEY HOPE SUSPENSE THRILLER series, comprising six books (and counting); the CAMILLE GRACE FBI SUSPENSE THRILLER series, comprising eight books (and counting); the HARLEY COLE FBI SUSPENSE THRILLER series, comprising eleven books (and counting); the KAYLIE BROOKS PSYCHOLOGICAL SUSPENSE THRILLER series, comprising five books (and counting); the EVE HOPE FBI SUSPENSE THRILLER series, comprising seven books (and counting); the DYLAN FIRST FBI SUSPENSE THRILLER series, comprising five books (and counting); the LAUREN LAMB FBI SUSPENSE THRILLER series, comprising five books (and counting); the KELSEY HAWK MYSTERY series, comprising five books (and counting); and the NORA PRICE MYSTERY series, comprising five books (and counting).

An avid reader and lifelong fan of the mystery and thriller genres, Kate loves to hear from you, so please feel free to visit www.kateboldauthor.com to learn more and stay in touch.

ISBN: 978-1-0943-9629-3

BOOKS BY KATE BOLD

NORA PRICE MYSTERY

CAN'T RUN (Book #1)
CAN'T HIDE (Book #2)
CAN'T ESCAPE (Book #3)
CAN'T SLEEP (Book #4)
CAN'T FORGET (Book #5)

KELSEY HAWK MYSTERY

DEAD INSIDE (Book #1)
DEAD RECKONING (Book #2)
DEAD TO ME (Book #3)
DEAD SILENCE (Book #4)
DEAD TO DAWN (Book #5)

ALEXA CHASE SUSPENSE THRILLER

THE KILLING GAME (Book #1)
THE KILLING TIDE (Book #2)
THE KILLING HOUR (Book #3)
THE KILLING POINT (Book #4)
THE KILLING FOG (Book #5)
THE KILLING PLACE (Book #6)

ASHLEY HOPE SUSPENSE THRILLER

LET ME GO (Book #1)
LET ME OUT (Book #2)
LET ME LIVE (Book #3)
LET ME BREATHE (Book #4)
LET ME FORGET (Book #5)
LET ME ESCAPE (Book #6)

CAMILLE GRACE FBI SUSPENSE THRILLER

NOT ME (Book #1)
NOT NOW (Book #2)
NOT WELL (Book #3)

NOT HER (Book #4)
NOT NORMAL (Book #5)
NOT AGAIN (Book #6)
NOT SAFE (Book #7)
NOT TODAY (Book #8)

HARLEY COLE FBI SUSPENSE THRILLER
NOWHERE SAFE (Book #1)
NOWHERE LEFT (Book #2)
NOWHERE TO RUN (Book #3)
NOWHERE LIKE THIS (Book #4)
NOWHERE GIRL (Book #5)
NOWHERE TO HIDE (Book #6)
NOWHERE CERTAIN (Book #7)
NOWHERE PURE (Book #8)
NOWHERE SOUND (Book #9)
NOWHERE SANE (Book #10)
NOWHERE TRUE (Book #11)

KAYLIE BROOKS PYSCHOLOGICAL SUSPENSE THRILLER
LAST BREATH (Book #1)
LAST CHANCE (Book #2)
LAST WISH (Book #3)
LAST SHOT (Book #4)
LAST MISTAKE (Book #5)

EVE HOPE FBI SUSPENSE THRILLER
IN HIS BLOOD (Book #1)
IN HIS SIGHTS (Book #2)
IN HIS REACH (Book #3)
IN HIS MIND (Book #4)
IN HIS WAY (Book #5)
IN HIS THOUGHTS (Book #6)
IN HIS DREAMS (Book #7)

DYLAN FIRST FBI SUSPENSE THRILLER
OUT OF REACH (Book #1)
OUT OF TOUCH (Book #2)
OUT OF TIME (Book #3)
OUT OF BOUNDS (Book #4)

OUT OF LUCK (Book #5)

LAUREN LAMB FBI SUSPENSE THRILLER
SOMETHING KNOCKING (Book #1)
SOMETHING CALLING (Book #2)
SOMETHING WRONG (Book 3)
SOMETHING DARK (Book #4)
SOMETHING TO HIDE (Book #5)

PROLOGUE

Where am I?

Miranda cowered on the ground and stared into the murky darkness of the unfamiliar room. She was on a dirt floor, the dust clinging to her nostrils, making her want to sneeze. But she held it back, not daring to make a sound.

Pain shot through her body as she tried to roll over from her side. She didn't know how long she'd been unconscious, or how long it had been since she'd locked up Mr. Creamy for the night. The overpowering stench of decay and the unbearable pain robbed her of any sense of time, but it felt like only minutes ago that she'd turned the key to the ice cream shop, thinking about nothing more than a chill Saturday night with her friends.

How quickly things had changed.

Now, she thought she might die.

She had no idea who had taken her. No idea at all. She'd barely turned to head to her car in the parking lot when someone had thrown a bag over her head. It had smelled like chemicals. Fertilizer.

She remembered the jolt of fear, the unbearable pain in her skull, and then … nothing.

Nothing, until now.

Miranda squinted into the gloom, barely spying a ladder fixed to the wall that led up to a hatch in the ceiling. She was in a dungeon, a tomb beneath the ground.

All at once, a dark thought occurred to her. *Nobody will ever find me here. I'll never leave this place alive.*

She forced that thought away, replacing it with a more hopeful one.

No. Dad. Mom. They have to be worried sick. They had to have called the police by now. There's got to be a search party looking for me.

She'd just settled into that hopeful thought when another one occurred to her.

Oh no. They just left for France. Dad had that business meeting.

Still, Miranda kept her eyes on the ceiling, hoping that at any minute, the hatch would open and her rescuers would storm this godforsaken tomb.

What happened was nothing of the sort. What happened was nothing at all. And bit by bit, she came to the bitter realization that there wouldn't be *anyone* coming to the rescue. Not in this dark hole in the ground, unfit for any living human.

She closed her eyes, and for the first time in a long while, she prayed.

A moment later, she heard the creaking of floorboards overhead. Footsteps, drawing closer. They fell silent directly above her head. Miranda's heart sped up.

Keep your eyes closed.

Panic and helplessness came over her. When she heard a flapping sound, like a carpet being pulled back, she felt sick with fear. Then, a weary, rasping croak announced the opening of the hatch.

Miranda's blood pounded in her ears and she swallowed the dust coating her dry throat. Whoever it was coming down that ladder, she had a feeling it wasn't her rescuer.

The man shuffled around the dark room as cigarette smoke began to mingle with the ever-present stench of decay.

Whoever is down here with me, he sure doesn't seem to be in a hurry.

Frantically, Miranda tried to think of something positive. That trip to Hawaii. Her boyfriend's suntanned face, his deep-set eyes, as blue as the sea in which they were paddling toward the horizon on their surfboards, trying to catch that perfect wave.

The images withered and died when she heard a strange mumbling. It sounded wrong. Inhuman, like some alien language. Miranda strained to listen.

Is that a man's voice?

Footsteps approached and stopped right in front of her. Miranda heard a soft laugh.

A man? Yes, definitely a man.

But something was still wrong about it. It sounded mechanical. Her body was shaking and it got even worse when he leaned down to her. He was so close now their faces almost touched.

Suddenly she felt a razor blade against her chin. Miranda kept her eyelids firmly shut as, inch by inch, the keen edge of the metal slid down her throat. The blade lingered at her larynx, then moved further down her cleavage and sliced off the top button of her blouse.

"No, please—please don't!" Miranda begged with her eyes closed as the blade cut off another button. She felt for sure she would then feel it cut right through the fabric in the center of her bra, and then she would be exposed to this madman. No longer could Miranda hold back her tears, which were now freely running down her cheeks.

"Pretty thing. Worthless thing. You have no idea how worthless you are. You're going to die now."

The voice speaking to her was so strange, so mechanical, almost robotic, that her eyes instantly flew open. Instantly, she regretted it. What she saw was horrific—a ghoul's face. She realized immediately that it was a mask, a wide-eyed, white-faced, frightening thing with deep red gashes in its forehead and cheeks.

As she stared in fear, the sudden pain of the first incision shot through her body. A deep gash throbbed in her skin. Followed by a second.

This is it. I'm going to die now.

Miranda squeezed her eyes closed and braced herself for another cut, for the life to drain from her body.

But nothing happened. The footsteps moved away. There was a creaking on the ladder, and the sound of the hatch closing. Then, silence.

Miranda's eyes snapped open. Gasping for breath, she quickly sat up, carefully probing the room with her eyes. She was alone again.

Where did he go?

She looked and realized—wonder of wonders—that he'd left the hatch open.

Miranda jumped to her feet, climbed the ladder, squeezed through the hatch, and emerged into a small, broken-down cabin.

She didn't take inventory. She saw the door, and she ran for it, blindly, pushing it open and escaping into the night. Ignoring the shrubs that scratched and tore at her bare legs, she hurried down an embankment, splashing into a riverbank, and pulled herself up. Dripping and ice-cold, she ran along the edge of it and let herself be swallowed by the night.

Only when the cottage was out of sight did she stop and rest her hands on her knees, gasping for breath.

Slowly her eyes grew accustomed to the dark, and in the pallid light of the moon, the outlines of bushes and trees emerged. It wasn't until her breathing had calmed that she noticed the sudden silence surrounding her. Then, a crack in the undergrowth. Startled, Miranda spun around.

Nothing. It was nothing.

Carefully, she patted her shorts, looking for her cell phone.

Gone. Both of her pockets were empty. *Dammit!*

Miranda looked back. Was he following her?

No. There was no one there.

Behind her, the forest rose like a black wall into the sky. Hesitantly, she turned around again and slipped between the trees, dodging them in the murky darkness until she reached a large clearing.

Where was she? She couldn't think.

There was that cracking sound again, much closer this time.

She strained into the night, searching for the one sight she did not want to see. That man's ghastly, grinning face.

Nothing.

And yet, she couldn't fight the feeling that he was there. Watching her. But who was he? In her mind, she thought of the creep. That's what the girls at Mr. Creamy called him. She'd served him half a dozen times. He was quiet but big, his face flat and square-shaped, eyes like slits, a nose that spread across his face. When he collected his order, he'd sit in a corner of the shop, just watching them while he licked at his vanilla cone.

Harmless, she'd told Vanessa, who'd joked he was going to kill them all one day.

If this was him …then she'd been wrong. So wrong.

Miranda jerked her head in all directions as she tried to look everywhere at once. Her eyes darted back and forth as if a pack of wolves were stalking her from the darkness of the forest, waiting for the perfect moment to pounce. Then she heard it again. That was no wolf. Those were footsteps, firm and purposeful, that had abruptly fallen silent again.

Only then did she hear the sound. A soft swishing, like cars on distant pavement. A road. From the constant swishing sound, it must be a busy road. A highway. Where was it?

As she squinted to see more clearly, something burst from the bushes. Miranda jumped back. She tripped on a branch and fell. She instantly sat up as the creature hopped off.

Just a rabbit, nothing but a scared little rabbit.

She brushed the dirt off her shorts, and there it was again: footsteps. Then, heavy breathing. There was someone behind her.

Miranda did not dare turn around. Instead, she ran for it, across the rolling meadows. Less than a hundred yards to the highway. She could see the lights of the cars now. On and on her legs carried her, as if on autopilot. When she finally reached the highway, she used her last bit of strength to pull herself up the embankment.

Miranda glimpsed headlights coming toward her. Not wasting another thought, she ran toward them. It was a small, banged-up pickup with square headlights, towing a small trailer. She waved her arms fiercely, and the truck went past her before slowing to a stop.

She rushed to the passenger-side door and banged fiercely on the window as it rolled down.

"Open up! Please!"

"All right, all right," the man with the trucker's cap said, reaching over to lift the lock. "What's the problem, little lady? You run into some trouble?"

She tugged on the door handle, looking over her shoulder in terror, sure the devil of a man was right on her tail, but saw only darkness. "Please. Police. I need to get to the police."

The man blinked. "Yeah. Of course. Right away."

Slamming the door behind her, she looked out the dirt-crusted window. There was no sign of him, and yet, she was sure he was there. Watching.

It was only when they pulled into the parking lot of the police station that she finally allowed herself to fall asleep.

CHAPTER ONE

Nora Price slumped in the chair and stared at her fingernails as if admiring a particularly good manicure.

Of course, she wasn't. Her nails were bloody, bitten to the quick, which was just how she liked them. Like some wild, starving animal, she was looking for any ragged piece of nail she'd missed.

A long silence would've crept in, if it weren't for that twangy sitar music being piped in from some unseen speaker. It was supposed to be calming, to get people to open up.

It wasn't working.

A moment later, Dr. Mathison started tapping her pen on her pad. Nora looked up to see her leaning forward, expectant. She had a professional updo, a businesslike pantsuit, and a thin, condescending smile that had rubbed Nora the wrong way from the moment they'd shaken hands twelve minutes ago.

Nora looked up at the clock on the wall. Twelve minutes and twenty-six seconds ago. Seven. Eight.

Oh, god. Time had never crept by so slowly. It was like it was going *backwards*.

"You were down there how long?"

Nora shrugged. "Like I said, I don't know. I don't know a lot."

"At what point in time did you realize your sister was gone?"

Nora sighed. She was beginning to feel like a broken record. "Like I said, I don't know."

Dr. Mathison leaned in to scribble some notes. This was exasperating. The woman was obviously new at this gig, asking questions that didn't matter, that no one had the answer to. No wonder it smelled like paint in here. Did someone just coat the walls in a nice shade of soothing vanilla? The office was typical. Soft ambient lighting, potted plants, paintings of rainbows and sunshine on the walls, comfy chairs with too many throw pillows. After this exercise, Nora would've loved to smother herself with one. Trying too hard to be cozy and welcoming, once again, to get people to open up.

Nora had been through all this before. She knew the drill.

"Seems like there are a lot of holes in that memory of yours," Dr. Mathison said, reading over her pad. Nora couldn't read it, but it was probably a whole lot of *I don't knows* and *beats mes*.

"And how do you feel about that?" Dr. Mathison prodded.

She found a spot on her thumb that hadn't been ravaged and gnawed on it, tasting blood. "Well, I feel just perfect, thanks for asking," she said brightly.

Dr. Mathison just stared, her brow wrinkled in disappointment. "Obviously, you're frustrated."

Nora sighed. But what did she expect? She'd just recounted her entire tragic past for the umpteenth time to the third psychiatrist in a year. It was starting to feel like something that had happened to someone else, not her.

And she knew this drill, too. They'd offer all these warm platitudes about forgiveness and moving on, and it wouldn't do one lick of good.

There was no moving on. Not yet.

But the FBI had rules. And one of their rules was that she needed to seek therapy for her many "issues."

So, here she was. "You think?"

Dr. Mathison smiled thinly. "You have a right to be, after … how long?"

Nora could've given the countdown. That it had been fourteen years, 212 days, thirteen hours, and six minutes—no, seven—since that man had first laid a hand on them. But that, she knew, would just be another thing for this lady to psychoanalyze. She'd write down: *Nora does not forget her trauma. Even for a second.*

And that would be right.

"Look," she said, tearing off a bloody half-moon of fingernail on her thumb. "I appreciate this. I know you're trying to help. But I'm good. I don't need the help."

"The FBI says—"

"Yes, I know what they say. But they don't know shit. Nothing you can say is going to turn my frown upside down. I've heard it all. And like I said, I'm *fine*."

Dr. Mathison looked down at the paper. "Your last doctor said you were suffering from PTSD, and—"

"I know what the doctor said."

"But you were resistant to help from him. From all of them."

She nodded. They'd put her through every kind of therapy imaginable. Probably would've gone for a lobotomy if those things still happened. All in the name of moving on, to get past the great big ball of hurt that squeezed her heart every time she had a second to think about it. Her employers said that in order to be an agent with them, she had to get better. Tame those demons. Move past it.

But the thing was, she didn't want to. Those demons were more like her friends now, helping her to ask the questions. Inspiring her to keep digging. Her past was a blanket full of holes. She wanted to stitch them.

And so she'd sit here, playing nice, and put in her time. But that was it.

"Except … it says here you have been to some hypnotists. Is that true?"

Nora nodded.

"So you do want to get better. How have things gone with that?"

It was a bad mistake, tearing off that last piece of nail. Her thumb was now bleeding all over the place. She crossed her arms to hide it from the doctor and stop herself from sucking on it.

"I'm here, aren't I?" She ran a finger over the edge of her thumbnail. It was wet with blood, probably enough to start dripping on the floor. She brought the thumb to her mouth and sucked the blood off anyway. "Anyhow, it wasn't to *get better*. It was to get answers."

"To what?"

Nora glared. She'd gone over this before.

"To shake free repressed memories, is that it? Of the incident?"

Now the doctor was looking at her like she was some crazy woman who'd gone to a psychic to communicate with her sister. Yes, sometimes she felt like she was at the end of her rope, but she hadn't gone that far. Not yet. Though she couldn't rule anything out, she wasn't going there. Doing so was like diving off a cliff, with no way of getting back.

Until she searched every possible avenue, she would not admit what everyone else already had.

Again, they were at an impasse.

Nora was done. She looked away.

"I can't help you unless you let me," Dr. Mathison said.

Nora let out a laugh. She'd heard that one about a thousand times. What, did all psychiatrists study from the same book?

This doc was definitely new. The ink on the Harvard diploma over her desk probably hadn't even dried yet. "You want to make my life better?"

She nodded. "Of course I do. That's what I'm here for. I want to help."

"Dr. Mathison," she said evenly, "if you really want to help me, you'll just sign the form that tells the FBI that I've put my hour in. And then we can all call it quits and go home."

Unfortunately, Dr. Mathison had other ideas. She was so new, she was still under the *I want to change the world!* delusion that she could actually help people. She flipped a page in her notebook and said, "Tell me about Sophia."

An image flashed in Nora's mind, then. Her sister, doing flips on the trampoline in the backyard, her blonde hair whipping behind her like a comet's tail. Cartwheels, round-offs, back handsprings. She'd been self-taught, never went to any of those fancy gym classes, but she could flip with the best of them, as if she belonged in the air.

An angel. That's what they compared her to. All the time, everywhere she went. So ethereal, she didn't belong among the normal people.

The week before the incident, Sophia had been so proud because as only a sophomore, she'd been made captain of the varsity cheerleading squad at their high school. Nora remembered her, constantly running through the grass barefoot, practicing routine after routine until her hands and feet were dark green. *Be aggressive. B-E aggressive. B-E-A-G-G-R-E-S-S-I-V-E!* Nora, always the wiseass who kept her feet firmly on the ground, had rolled her eyes and joked that that was the only way Sophia would ever learn to spell the word.

Of course, it hadn't been true. Though Nora, a year younger, had always been thought of as the brain, Sophia was a lot smarter than anyone gave her credit for. But her beauty and grace overshadowed everything else. She was the type of girl who attracted attention. Women stopped her on the street to tell her how beautiful she was. Men—even much older men—constantly flirted with her. Their dad put rules in that they couldn't date until they were sixteen—precisely because Sophia had gotten her first invitations, from boys in her school to fully grown men their father's age, starting at twelve.

Nora hadn't gotten a single one, even by fourteen. And so she had been jealous. She just knew that when she entered her freshman year of high school, she was going to be known as "Sophia's sister."

The nameless, lesser one.

And then the two of them had been walking home from their summer job at the breakfast place, and everything changed. Because Sophia was running late for cheer practice, they decided to take a shortcut through the woods.

Cue the holes in her memory.

It was funny, she remembered everything about that morning. The two of them ran JP's like it was their own place. JP, the owner, was too old to go in, so he lived upstairs. He'd given them the keys, so they opened and locked up on their own. Nora flipped pancakes and Sophia waited tables, and they split the tips. She remembered Sophia carefully spreading the dollar bills out on the counter. They'd each made thirteen dollars, but there was change, which Sophia had taken. "I deserve it. You're lucky, all you do is stand in front of a stove all morning. I have to deal with all the creeps."

And they were creeps. Mostly crotchety old men who'd been coming to JP's every morning for fifty years. They'd always say, "Come warm up my coffee, sweetie," to her, just to get close to her beauty or look at her butt in those tight workout shorts. Yet Sophia had always delivered service with a smile, and even flirted with them, too, a bit, to get better tips.

So Nora had agreed, she deserved it.

But that didn't stop her from secretly hating her sister and wishing that just once, something bad would happen to her.

And then, just like that … something bad did happen.

Nora blinked out of the memory to find Dr. Mathison staring at her, expectant. "She was …" she started, her mouth moving in different shapes as she tried to select the answer. *Everyone's favorite. My best friend. The bane of my existence.* She finally swallowed and said, "Beautiful. Everyone loved her."

"What is your last memory of her?"

Nora's eyes narrowed as she thought of Sophia, walking ahead of her through the woods. She'd looked back at her, pissed. *Come on. Move your slow butt. I don't want to be late. They're waiting for me.*

Nora had gritted her teeth, watching her perfect blonde ponytail swishing ahead of her. It looked like sunshine. Nora's own hair was too short, mousy, dark.

My last memory of her was how much I hated her.

She bit her lip to keep it from trembling. Then she stretched her mouth into a smile. "I'm not going down memory lane with you, Doc. I've been there enough, and I'd prefer to stay in the present."

"But you agree that you'll never heal until—"

"I agree I'll never heal," she said, rising to her feet and checking the clock. "And I'm good with it. I've made peace with my crooked, diseased mind. How about we call it a day?"

Dr. Mathison straightened and looked at the clock. "I think we can make progress if you sit and tell me—"

“I’ve made a lot of progress,” she muttered, walking to the door. “You can write on the form you submit to the bureau that I’m feeling loads better, and it’s all your doing. Okay?”

“Hold on—”

By that time, she’d reached the door, and she pulled it open just as the doctor had launched herself from her seat to go after her. The waiting room was full. The receptionist and all the patients must’ve heard the doctor’s voice raised in alarm, because they all looked up from their phones and magazines as Nora sailed past them, slamming the door behind her.

The receptionist jumped up. “Wait, you have to—”

“Send the bill to the bureau with my compliments,” she said, and made a swift exit, back to a life with more questions than answers.

And Nora Price was perfectly fine with that. It was where she belonged.

CHAPTER TWO

There was no air conditioning in the cramped subway car, and it was almost rush hour, so by the time the T arrived at her station outside of Boston, Nora was practically swimming in sweat. She stepped out of the car into eighty-degree heat, peeling her sticky clothes away from her body and gulping air that, for once, didn't smell like BO.

An old man with a suitcase stopped in front of her, grinning. "You should smile," he said, not unkindly.

"And you should learn to mind your own business," she muttered, turning away from him. He let out a hmph as she hurried down the ramp.

Creeps, she thought.

At times like these, she felt she understood her sister better than she ever had before that day. Sophia *hated* the attention of men, especially strangers, but she would've done as he asked, like a trained monkey. She always wanted to make everyone happy. She'd smile, and they'd compliment her on how beautiful she was, and she'd eat it up.

But that was what had doomed them both. Not all men were creeps, Nora knew. But it only took one. You never could tell which was which. And they'd crossed the wrong one.

That had been one good thing about having Sophia Price as a sister. She took *all* attention off Nora—even the bad.

So Nora could only think that that was what had happened that day. Sophia had gotten the brunt of their kidnapper's bad attention, and as a result, Nora had lived.

She shuddered at the thought as she made her way down the street, past the many people sitting out on the front stoops of their homes, enjoying the warm weather. She ignored them all. Blackburn County was where she'd grown up, and where the incident had happened. She'd never liked the place, even before the incident, but now, the short walk made her skin crawl. Her parents had never moved away, which always shocked people. The abandoned house where it happened, a few blocks over, had been razed, replaced by a little park with a statue of an angel in the center, surrounded by purple flowers. It had a plaque that said "In Memory of Sophia Price" and had a picture of her, wearing her cheerleading uniform and holding their pet dog Snoopy. The park was called "Sophia's Place."

Nora had never visited it. Not even for the dedication, which happened five years later, after the Blackburn County town council had raised enough money for the memorial and local businesses had chipped in for the work. She made the excuse that she was busy in college, but that wasn't true. She could've easily gone.

She agreed with keeping Sophia's memory alive. But not with a memorial.

Because as far as Nora was concerned, Sophia wasn't dead. A memorial wouldn't help find her. The only thing that would do that was action.

As she was about to cross the road to head to Smith Street, her eyes caught on someone walking ahead of her.

She was tall and impossibly skinny. Pale blonde hair, bouncing on her shoulders.

It brought Nora back to that day in the woods, following her sister and wishing she could have hair so angelic, so shiny …

The girl on the sidewalk ahead was with a tall boy in a T-shirt and jeans. She wearing a short, form-fitting belly shirt and tight shorts, the style of today. Sophia loved wearing baggy jeans and tops, but still, that hair …

Without fully realizing what she was doing, Nora skipped into a run. The girl was heading toward her parents' house. Maybe she'd finally gotten free from wherever she'd been, and was now on her way to them. Nora's heart practically burst. How happy her parents would be! And Nora could tell them that she was right—*see, I told you she wasn't dead!*

"Sophia?" she called, but the girl did not turn around.

She picked up her pace, finally catching up with her as she crossed into the street. But even as she put a hand on the woman's bare arm, she realized it was a mistake.

This girl wasn't nearly as beautiful. When she turned around, confused, all the features on her face were wrong. Nora's spirits plummeted as the woman regarded her.

"What's going on?" she grouched.

"Sorry," Nora said, taking a step back. "I thought you were someone else."

The girl looked at her like she was insane before heading off. The boy she was with said something and wrapped an arm around her, and she giggled.

Nora watched her go, feeling stupid. That girl was all of fifteen, the same age Sophia was when the incident occurred. If Sophia were alive today, she'd be thirty-three. No matter how many times she told herself that, it never seemed to sink in.

But it was better than the other thing she saw sometimes.

Him.

No, she didn't know what her captor looked like. But sometimes she'd have a feeling, or hear a voice, or see something silly, like a watch chain or a certain kind of wide-toothed smile, and she'd go board-stiff, with shivers traveling up and down the length of her spine. They were like fragments from different broken items—impossible to put together into a whole.

This girl, though, was clearly not Sophia. Not even close. Mathison was probably right. She did need help.

Not from that quack, though. She'd never go back there again.

Just get a grip. You can do this, Nora thought, just as a horn blared and brakes squealed.

She jumped and quickly ran out of the street, then hurried the rest of the way to her childhood home, thinking of the last time Sophia had jogged down these steps, dangling her apron at her side, late for that fateful last shift at JP's.

*

When Nora arrived, her mother was wrapped in an afghan, and the air conditioner in the window was buzzing, like always, at full blast. Her feet, in knit booties, were propped in a V on a velvet-covered ottoman. The green leather recliner was bobbing along with the rhythm of her snores. The television was set to the local news channel, and the volume was cranked so high that Nora's inner ear throbbed.

She twisted the dial to OFF and massaged her mother's shoulder gently. Monica Price's head drooped to the side, one eye opened halfway, and a glazed pupil focused on her.

"Hi, Mom," Nora said, kneeling beside the chair. "How are you today?"

She was now fully awake, but still disoriented. Groggily, she said, "Is it lunchtime already?"

"I'm early," Nora told her.

She smiled, and her loose dentures clicked into place. "I thought you had a doctor's appointment downtown."

"Yeah. It didn't go very well."

The leathery wrinkles on her face compressed in a look of sheer disappointment. Monica Price wasn't even sixty yet, but the stress of losing her firstborn had done a number on her, and she wore the scars on every last inch of her body. She kicked up out of the recliner and shook her head. "I think you've gone to every doctor in the city. Why can't you just—"

"Mom, I don't need it," she said, following the smell of something delicious toward the kitchen. "What's for lunch?"

Nora's father, Dan Price, stood in front of the stove, sampling. He raised a finger to his lips as he chewed.

"Caught you," she whispered, just as her mother said, "Sausage and peppers. If your father is in there, tell him to get out! There won't be enough for the three of us if he keeps doing his taste test!"

Nora smiled conspiratorially at him and reached into the pot with a spoon to have a taste of the sauce.

"So the doc's really didn't go well?" her father said with concern.

"It's the same thing, Dad," she said with a shake of her head. "I need to do it for the bureau. Whether it helps me or not. But I can't just sit there and listen to them drone on about 'moving on and moving up' and 'tomorrow is another day.' I can't believe they're being paid to spout that crap."

"I don't know … it could be helpful."

"Helpful? What could possibly be helpful about it?"

He tilted his head. "Maybe if you actually listened, you'd learn something."

She sighed. She'd been over this time and time again with them. They wanted to move on from Sophia. And, when the park was constructed, they had. Or at least, they did a good job of pretending. They'd packed all her things into a corner of the attic, except for a single shelf in the bookcase, where they kept her obituary and a memorial plaque given to them by the Rotary Club, after the park had been dedicated.

But Nora flat-out refused to give up that easily. Until she had the evidence in her hands, she'd never believe that her sister was gone.

"Dad …" she began, a warning.

He shrugged and regarded her with watery, sad eyes. "You know, when you were twelve, you wanted to be a doctor. That was all you talked about …"

She looked into the pot of sausages and sighed. They'd been over this before. Yes, back then she'd wanted to do vital work, and she saw medicine as the most vital of all.

To her parents, it seemed like she'd suddenly made a one-eighty after high school, deciding she had to go into law enforcement. She'd applied the moment she was ready for a job at the FBI. It might have come out of left field to her parents, but to Nora, it had been stewing ever since she emerged from that basement alive.

She wanted to be the one to put creeps like that in jail. To her, that was the most vital work of all.

And she'd done well at it.

Five years on the force. Thirty-two creeps in prison because of her.

If she had to guess, that was the only reason why the director hadn't taken away her badge. Her record spoke for itself. So what if she'd omitted a few details on her application? It wasn't her fault that their lengthy background check hadn't uncovered her traumatic past. Besides, her boss, Special Agent Durham, knew that she was a damn good agent, and why? Because she'd experienced that trauma. Because she cared more than all of the agents in her field office put together.

She got things done. That was all that mattered.

Monica Price shuffled into the kitchen then, looking even more beaten than usual. She gave her husband a warning look and said, "Set the table. I've got to take my pills."

When she left, Nora reached into the pantry to pull down the old, chipped, flowered plates, relics from her childhood. When they were a family of four, Monica Price used to run marathons. She loved to hike and be outdoors. She was the picture of health, always making sure they minded what they put in their bodies and providing three square meals a day. Now, the Price medicine cabinet was like a pharmacy counter, full of every anti-anxiety and depression medication known to man. Every time Monica Price tried to go off them, she wound up spiraling again.

So, no matter how many times her parents insisted that they'd moved on, Nora refused to believe it. This wasn't moving on. Far from it.

"She doesn't look great," Nora whispered to her father as she folded napkins. "What happened?"

"Oh, she visited your sister's grave this morning," Dan Price said quietly, shaking his head. "You know how she gets when she does that."

Nora figured it was something like that. And yet every week, her mother always had to stop in. "I don't know why she puts herself through that," she grumbled.

He gave her a sharp look. "You haven't been there in a while. Have you?"

She rolled her eyes to the ceiling. In truth, she hadn't been there in years. It was like the park. Worthless. The grave was empty. Having a place like that to pay respects to Sophia might have been fine for her parents, but to Nora, it seemed like a waste. If there was no body, there was a chance she could still be alive. And yet no one ever said that anymore. It was as if they'd all forgotten that.

"Right. And I'm not going there," she said, her tone just as sharp. "I'm not giving up. You know how—"

"I know you're only making things worse," her mother said, standing in the door. "Somehow, you keep bringing this up. It's over. Sophia's gone. We've all accepted that, and—"

"Moved on?" Nora scoffed. "Mom. You think this is moving on? You say it is, but I know there is part of you crying at that empty grave, wondering where your daughter is, if not in that casket. That's why you don't sleep, why you take every pill in the book. Why you've never left this town. It's because as much as you've tried to convince yourself with pretty memorials and shrines to her, you don't have closure. You can't help wondering, just like me."

Monica stared at her. "You're wrong! Why did you come to this house, if only to dredge up—"

"No," her father said quietly. "No, we can not, and will not, keep wondering. You know why?"

She knew from the look on her parents' faces that she had gone too far. All she'd wanted was a lazy afternoon meal with her family. Not this. She wished she could take it back, to stop talking about it. Instead, her father kept going.

"Because it would drive us mad. Which is where you are headed, Charlene. Don't you see that? That is why the FBI has you in therapy. Because you are driving yourself insane."

She swallowed the bile in her throat. He was right. But then again, if she didn't hold out hope, who would?

She was about to tell him that when her phone rang. It was Durham, at the field office in Boston. No doubt Mathison had ratted her out and told him the truth about their disastrous first appointment, and now she was in hot water.

Cringing, she held up a finger and mouthed that she had to take it. Then she went out to the foyer, pressing the phone against her ear and bracing for the shitstorm. "Look, it just wasn't the right fit," she said to him before he could get a word in.

"That's nothing new," he said offhandedly, and she could tell there was a smile behind his hard words. That was one thing about Mick Durham. As messed up as she was, he never seemed to hold it against her. He followed protocol to a fault, but he always gave her the benefit of the doubt.

"The woman was a definite newbie," Nora said, looking around the foyer, her eyes settling on a photograph of Sophia at her middle-school graduation. She'd been thirteen, the age when most kids look awkward or gangly, but Sophia had never gone through that stage. Even then, she'd been angelic. "I think I need someone with a little bit more experience to sift through all my skeletons."

"Hmm," he said. "Which one was she?"

Something occurred to Nora at that moment. "Wait. You didn't get the report from her yet?"

"Not yet. I was calling about a case. Snyder's already been apprised, but I wanted him to bring you in specifically."

She blinked. "And why is that?"

"It's a kidnapping. A young girl was last seen at her after-school job. She may have been kidnapped."

The last word was barely out of his mouth before she said, "I'll be right there."

She ended the call and went into the kitchen, where her parents were just sitting down to lunch. "I have to go. It's a case."

A case that sounds a lot like Sophia's, she thought, but didn't say it. They'd moved on, or at least, that was what they wanted to believe, and what good was it to bring it up again?

CHAPTER THREE

Nora actually managed to smile when she climbed into the car that was idling in front of her apartment building.

Jason Snyder had always had that effect on her.

"You look like shit," he said with a thin smile.

"And you look worse." She spied the coffee in the cup holder nearest to her. *Bless him.* Lifting it to her nose, she inhaled the rich scent of the beans, laced with hazelnut-flavored creamer. Her favorite. "What have you been doing, prowling the bars for women stupid enough to get with your ugly ass?"

"I'll have you know, I actually had a taker last night, and she wasn't even close to hideous. Nina."

Nora rolled her eyes. Nina. Of course. "She actually saw your bedroom and didn't run away?"

His brows rose in amusement. "No. Incredibly."

That was incredible. Jason Snyder was a die-hard baseball fan, and actually had his bedroom decorated to look like Fenway Park. He even had one wall painted green, to signify the Green Monster. Add to that the Sox memorabilia he had all over his bachelor pad … it was a bit of a woman's worst nightmare. "Was she drunk out of her mind?"

He frowned. "Possibly."

"Hmm. Are you going to see her again?"

He scoffed. "Just who do you think I am?"

She snorted. Jason liked to play the part of the ultimate lothario, stalking young women everywhere, but Nora was sure that one day, he'd settle down if he found the right woman. But for now, he was married to his job. He was just as committed to it as she was, though for entirely different reasons. Jason Snyder had dreamed all his life of this—he'd gone from the Navy to the FBI, always in the interest of fighting the bad guys. It was his number one passion. Number two was the Sox. For now, women were nothing more than a diversion.

That was what made him a good partner. He took nothing in his life as seriously as the job. And he was loyal as hell, almost to a fault. From the moment she'd sat down with him five years ago, she knew she'd found her partner. They just clicked. Not romantically, though.

Sometimes he felt like the brother she'd never had. The sibling she'd lost. Not a perfect fit to take Sophia's place, but a reasonable substitute.

She sipped her coffee as he took off toward midtown. "So what do we have, and why did Durham seem so hot on this?"

He motioned to the file, tucked between the seat and the center console. "Check it out. A girl named Miranda Forster. She showed up on Route 3 in a state, banging on some passerby's car. She claims to have been kidnapped."

That name rang a very clear bell. One couldn't live in the Boston area without hearing the name Forster. "Of those Forsters?"

"That's right. The bean dynasty."

Nora opened the folder to view a photograph of a pretty blonde girl in a hospital gown. She was pale, with bloodshot, faraway eyes and a deep scratch on her cheekbone. Instantly, her mind cycled back to Sophia.

Billionaires probably didn't care how they'd gained success, but Nora had to wonder if any of the younger Forsters had ever had a hard time in grade school, being known as Bean Royalty. Forster's Baked Beans was practically a household name, and they'd had a factory near the Back Bay for over a hundred years. She was sure there were probably a lot of flatulence jokes being tossed their way, despite the fact that their faces always graced the newspaper's society pages.

But this girl didn't look like a spoiled princess. She looked very much like any ordinary teen, skinny and anxious. The bruises on her face spoke to a hard ordeal. Nora wished she could hug her. "She said she was kidnapped leaving her after-school job?"

"Yeah, she works at the Mr. Creamy on Walnut." The classic rock on the radio turned to an announcer's voice, so Snyder turned it down. "But the family name is not the only reason Durham's so hot on this."

She turned the pages of the file, understanding quickly dawning. "He thinks this might be connected to the other two murders?"

Snyder nodded. "It checks out. Similar description; young, pretty female. Same area."

Nora paged through the file, growing more and more interested. Two murdered girls had been found outside Blackburn County that summer, and the case had hit Nora a little too close to home, bringing back memories of Sophia at every turn. Especially since they weren't able to catch the creep, and all leads had gone cold. But if this girl was a survivor of the killer, they had a new opening. A hot lead like this was just what they needed to finally put this case to bed.

Not that it was a done deal. After all, Nora had been a survivor, and had given the police every bit of information she could remember. And still, their kidnapper and Sophia had never been found. The holes in Nora's memory were just too vast. Maybe this girl would prove to be a better witness.

"The police talk to her? What is she saying? Does she remember anything?"

He nodded. "A hell of a lot, apparently. She's a trouper. Scared as she is, she gave them a description of the man she thinks did it, and they have a sketch."

Nora raised an eyebrow. Not only was it promising, it was impressive. This Miranda Forster had to have been made of some pretty strong stuff. Nora always beat herself up for having been too weak. Her mind had blocked out entirely the most terrible parts of her ordeal. But not this girl, apparently.

Looking out the window, she noted that they were just around the corner from the hospital. Good. She had a lot of questions, and it seemed this witness might do a better job than she had.

She swallowed the lump in her throat as she thought about her own failures, once again, for the millionth time in her life.

"Look," Snyder said, his voice uncharacteristically serious as he pulled into the roundabout for the hospital's front entrance. "I know what you're thinking. And if you want to take a breather at any time …"

She gave him a tired look. Most of the time, it was a blessing that the two of them got along better than peanut butter and jelly. But at times like these, when her confidence was on shaky terrain, she wished he couldn't see straight into her soul. "I'm fine," she said, her voice harder than she'd intended.

"You sure?" he said, and she knew that he knew it was a lie.

She looked into his eyes. Contrary to what she always said to him, he never looked like hell. Sure, he was a little pale, and his razor burn was always evident on his jaw. At thirty, he still had freckles, which made him look more like a teenager who'd practiced shaving with his dad's razor and forgot the shaving cream. But he had nice blue eyes and a pleasant face, one that people couldn't help but like and trust.

"If I'm not, I'll give you the signal," she said lightly, reaching for the door handle.

His eyes narrowed. "The signal?"

"Yeah. I'll flail on the ground before curling into a fetal position. That's your sign to get me out of there." She winked and opened the door. When he followed, looking after her with doubt, she said, “Come on, Agent, and stop worrying about me. We have a victim to interview.”

CHAPTER FOUR

The Blackburn County Regional Hospital wasn't as big as the sprawling complexes in the heart of the city, but it was busy nonetheless. The halls of the ICU were just as sparse and cold, filled with medical personnel shuttling between rooms to perform their assorted duties. As Nora stepped around a janitor who was busily cleaning up some undefined, foul-smelling puddle in the middle of the hallway, Jason leaned into her. "This is why I never became a doctor."

She laughed. "Is it?" It was particularly hilarious because some of the things they'd seen were far more unpleasant. But Jason always seemed to have a bit of a weak stomach. "I'm sure there are *many* other things that would've stood in the way of you becoming a doctor."

"If you're talking about brain cells, I'll have you know I graduated summa cum laude from BU," he said, a fact he reminded her of at least once a week.

"Right. I'll believe that one when I see your transcripts."

"I told you. Any day of the week. I'll show you," he said as they made their way down the hall. "Come on over."

"And I thought BU was actually selective. Makes me wonder if the admissions committee was drunk that …" She trailed off as they reached the room. From the door, she could see a girl's pale feet in the hospital bed, and a bit of the patterned gown. Her toenails were painted a bright pink.

As Nora moved forward, she saw the long blonde hair, and instantly, her mind cycled back to one of her most overplayed fantasies, something she'd envisioned almost every moment, back when Sophia first went missing: They'd get the call that she'd been found and was being treated at a local hospital. They'd arrive, with flowers and gifts, to find Sophia sitting up in bed, just as beautiful as always. They'd all hug, become the perfect family, and from that moment, Nora would vow never to wish bad on her sister ever again.

Of course, that never happened. But looking at young Miranda Forster, sitting up in bed, chewing on a slice of burnt wheat toast and watching some talk show on the television tethered to the wall, Nora couldn't help but mark the similarities. The pale skin, the twiglike limbs, the long, sunshine-blonde hair. When her eyes turned toward Nora, expectant, there was a little bit of annoyance in them, too, the way Sophia had always regarded her when their mom asked her to let Nora tag along.

Nora hovered in the doorway, speechless for a moment, until Jason maneuvered past her and filled in the silence. "Miranda Forster?"

She nodded and pulled her legs into crisscross-applesauce, pulling her gown out over her knees. "More detectives?"

"We're from the FBI, actually," he said, simultaneously flashing his badge and pulling one of the chairs away from the window toward her. "Jason Snyder and my partner, Nora Price. How are you doing?"

She shrugged. "Fine. I'll be better when my parents get here. They were in Paris when it happened."

"I know you've answered questions for the police. You mind answering a few more for us? We know you've been through hell, so we won't keep you long."

Nora had to smile at how good he was. It might have been the gentle voice, the red hair, the freckles, but he never let female victims think he was one of *them*. One of the bad guys, the type who could do horrendous things to those weaker than him. He had such a disarming way about him, something she'd felt the moment she stepped into this room with him.

It was definitely a gift, and the girl responded as Nora expected. She nodded. "Of course."

Since she couldn't yet trust her voice to betray her and show how off her game this situation made her feel, Nora stood back and let her partner begin the questioning. "Miranda—may I call you Miranda?" When she nodded, he continued. "I know you've done this before, but would you mind starting from the beginning and telling us your version of the events that took place?"

She shrugged. "Sure. It's like I said. I'm the closer at Mr. Creamy's on Walnut. Since it's never very busy at night, I work there alone. That night, I locked up, and I was just about to go to my car when someone threw a bag over my head."

Nora turned pages in the file as she spoke. She wasn't sure she wanted to hear this, because though she remembered nothing of her own kidnapping, she was sure it went something like that. She'd been taken, and ended up somewhere, tethered, where she thought she might die. "You got a good look at your captor?" she asked.

She nodded. "Well, it was dark in the basement, and he was wearing a mask."

"A ski mask, you mean?"

"No, like a Halloween mask. Like a white face with red gashes in the eyes and mouth. It looked gross. And it had one of those weird voice changers in it, distorting the voice. At first I thought he was speaking a different language, but then I realized it was a machine."

"What did he say?"

"Just that he was going to kill me. I didn't see him when he put the bag over my head. But I'm pretty sure I know who he was. He used to come into Mr. Creamy's and stare at all us girls as we worked. He was a customer."

"Do you have a name?" Snyder asked.

She shook her head. "No. I just provided the description of the customer to the police officers."

Nora flipped through the file to find the police sketch. If ever a man could be called a creep just by looks, it was this one. His face was altogether square, and some of his features—his eyes, his nose—were too big, giving him a cartoonish look. But there was nothing funny about him. The eyes were dead, and downright evil. Long, stringy hair only seemed to amplify his bald spot. Nora suppressed a shudder and showed the photograph to Jason.

"Guy that looks like that should be easy to find," Snyder said, giving Miranda a smile. "You're a real observant girl."

She shrugged. "I want to catch that jerk."

"All right, keep going," Snyder said, giving Nora a warning look. Or maybe it was a sympathetic look. Whatever it was, he wanted the rest of the story out. And as much as she knew it had to come out …Nora wasn't sure she could hear it. "Tell us more."

Miranda nodded. "I tried to fight, but they knocked me out. When I woke up, I was in what felt like a hole in the ground, with like, a hatch. It was all dusty and I couldn't breathe."

Something tickled at the back of Nora's throat. She remembered the outline of a door, framed in light. So much darkness. Being cold and cramped, and not knowing where she was. Trying to call for her sister but tasting an oily rag stuffed into her mouth.

But most of all, she remembered the fear of not knowing what the next few moments would bring.

"Go on," Jason said, just as Nora's hands started to shake, and she dropped the folder.

He glanced back at her as she stooped to pick up the strewn papers, trying not to comprehend the words Miranda was saying. And as much as she tried to tune them out, each one seemed to pluck at something inside her, making her every nerve go haywire.

"A guy came down the hatch and started to poke at me with a knife. I don't know what happened, but he left the hatch open, and I ran."

Crouched there in front of the stacked papers, Nora felt those words in her bones. The uncertainty. The dread of what was to come. She wasn't sure how she had escaped—maybe it was her captor's momentary lapse in judgment, but she'd managed to get free.

Jason asked a question, but Nora wasn't listening. All she heard was Miranda's voice. "Yes. It was a cabin in the woods. Off of Route Three, by where it forks off at the convenience store."

Props to Miranda for remembering. Nora, on the other hand, had come up with very little, which was why the police canvassed the woods outside Blackburn County for nearly three weeks, finding absolutely nothing. She remembered running, screaming, through a forest dark as pitch, not sure where she was headed. For hours or days, she couldn't tell. She remembered the relief as she finally ran into the arms of someone who would keep her safe. How could a thing be so hazy and yet create emotions and feelings that still cut so deep?

"I didn't stop until I got to the road and that man in the pickup stopped for me. I asked him to take me to the police, and he did."

Slowly, Nora rose, her heart beating out of her chest. She couldn't remember the name of the person she'd finally run to. She couldn't remember where she'd run, or for how long. The only thing she did remember, with absolute clarity, was the tortured screams of her sister. She'd never heard Sophia sound like that before. So scared, so lost, so helpless … it was that sound that echoed in her nightmares, until she woke up, screaming along with her.

A hand clamped around Nora's forearm, stirring her from her thoughts. Snyder's eyes were on hers, rimmed with concern. "Can I speak with you outside?" he said, motioning to the door.

She followed him out.

The moment they were out in the hallway, he turned to her and leaned in. "You okay?"

"Of course," she said, with more confidence than she felt.

"Are you sure about that?"

"Yes, why would you even ask?" she said, looking past him, into the room. "We're getting good stuff there. She's obviously got the location down and the description. We've really hit the jackpot with her. She's like a star wit—"

"Because you were shaking," he said, pressing his lips together.

Shaking. Had she been? Possibly. There were so many emotions inside her to keep at bay, so many reactions she had to work to control. The therapist before Dr. Mathison had told her that if she didn't find a healthy way to deal with them, she might lash out one day, hurting everyone around her. She hated to think of herself as a volcano or a ticking time bomb. But maybe that was just what she was.

"I'm fine. Just … low blood sugar."

He sighed and looked toward the door. No, he didn't believe that, either. Then he reached into the pocket of his blazer, took her hand, and put something inside it.

A granola bar.

"You really should eat breakfast. Most important meal of the day," he said to her, before turning to go back inside. "Come on. Let's find out more about this cabin in the woods. I think that should be our next stop."

CHAPTER FIVE

Nora munched on the granola bar, playing a Chopin nocturne in her head while Jason Snyder asked the questions.

So far, she wagered it was doing its magic. It was keeping her still, since Jason never looked up at her as he took his notes. Good thing he was taking those notes, because she had no clue what Miranda Forster was describing. She made hand motions, her eyes growing wide, and nodded every so often, so Nora assumed it was the scene of the crime. The dark, damp wood walls, the dirt floor, the smell of decay … all of it.

She didn't have to imagine it. She'd lived it.

And she knew that if she had to *relive* it, she'd be shaking again.

When Jason finally stood and pocketed his notepad, Nora turned off the music in her head and stood, too. She shook the victim's hand and smiled at her. "Thanks for the information."

They walked out, and she knew her partner was on to her. Nora wasn't one to fade into the background during a questioning, unless …

"Thanks for taking the reins there," she said softly as they headed toward the elevator. "That low blood sugar's a killer."

"Of course. You feeling better now?"

"Much."

When they reached the elevator, he dug into his pocket and pulled out the notepad. He flipped it open and handed it to her. She read it as the elevator dinged to announce they'd reached the lobby. *Check out woods to the east of Blackburn County Gas-n-Sip.*

"You know I can't read your chicken-scratch," she said, just to tease him.

"Uh-huh." Again, he didn't believe her. "You ever been out there? I fill up there once a week. There's a median on Route Three so if the car she flagged down was headed north, it stands a good chance the cabin she ran from was to the east. She wouldn't jump the median to flag down a car, right?"

Nora nodded slowly at his proud, smug expression. "Well, aren't you brilliant."

"I know. I told you. Sharp as a tack," he said, as the doors opened.

As they stepped out, a woman in a suit, with her hair in a bun, nearly collided with them. She dropped her file, and the pages went scattering along the polished tile floor. The woman let out an exasperated whine.

"Shoot, let me help you with that," Snyder said, reaching down to help her collect them. Nora, too, stooped down, grabbing handfuls and pulling them together, glad she wasn't the only klutz in that hospital today.

"It's fine, it's fine, I'm just late," the woman said as Nora looked at the top paper.

She noticed the name on top as the woman took the page from her. "Miranda Forster? Is that who you're here to see?"

The woman nodded. "Yes …"

Snyder said, "We were just up there, interviewing her. We're with the FBI. We've been assigned to her case."

"Oh!" The woman was quite young, probably in her late twenties, but the pantsuit and severe bun made her look older. She was pretty, though, and had the long, elegant features of a dancer. Nora noticed it especially as she took the woman's hand, with its long, slender fingers. "I'm Tess Benson. Dr. Tess Benson. I'm Miranda's therapist. Actually, I'm the therapist for the Forster family, but I used to see Miranda when she was younger."

Jason shook her hand, brow raised. "Wow. How'd someone so young get a gig like that?"

She laughed, tucking a lock of cinnamon hair behind her ear and adjusting her glasses. "I'm not as young as I look, but, well, our families grew up together. And I'm sure you must know, trauma runs in the Forster family."

Nora and Jason exchanged a look. "No …what do you mean?"

She looked up and down the hallway before motioning them to a corner and lowering her voice. "Well, Ben Forster, Miranda's father, had another family before Miranda. He had a son and a wife. Well, he left his first wife, Ann, for Miranda's mom, and there was a huge scandal about it. It was a messy divorce, and the son, who was only about six or seven at the time, wanted to live with his father. One night, when Miranda was only about two or three, Ann sneaked into the house with a knife. She killed the boy."

Nora's eyes widened and she looked at Jason. "No kidding. So you've been their therapist since then?"

"Yes. Miranda's had several therapists over the years. She's been through a lot." She shook her head. "That was why I came running when I heard. She's been working so hard to have a normal life, and making great strides. And now this."

A sick feeling crept into Nora's gut. If the public knew about this already, the media would soon come swarming, making their job all the more difficult. "And how did you hear? It's not on the news yet."

"No. I stopped by this afternoon to pick up some papers from Mr. Forster—he's out of town—and one of the housekeepers told me about it. I came right over." She bit at her lip. "Have you seen her? Is she all right?"

"She's better than most would be," Jason said.

"I guess she would be," Dr. Benson said, almost to herself. "Enough bad things happen to a person, they tend to become numb to it."

Nora clenched her teeth. After everything she'd gone through, she'd have considered numbness a blessing. But apparently, she wasn't there yet. And if more trauma was what it took, she didn't ever want to be.

"Well, I hope she was helpful to you," the therapist said with a curious look their way. "Whoever did this ..."

"Very helpful," Nora said.

"Very?" Dr. Benson's eyes went wide. "She knows who did it?"

"Well, not for sure," Jason explained. "But she helped produce a sketch of the man she thinks is responsible, and we have a good idea where he took her. So we're hoping it won't be long before we have some answers."

"Oh," the therapist said, once again smoothing her hair behind her ear. "Well, good luck. If you excuse me, I really need to get to my patient and see if she needs anything."

"Of course," Nora said, and the woman rushed into the open elevator just as the doors began to close.

As they walked back to the car, Jason had his nose in his phone. "What are you looking at?" she asked him when he nearly collided with a woman in a wheelchair.

He pointed at the screen. "I thought I remembered something about the incident with Ben Forster. It was before our time. Check it out."

He handed her his phone and clicked open the doors to the car. She slid into the passenger's seat and read the story:

Boston woman convicted of killing her 7-year-old son just days after losing full custody of him

Boston—A woman who sneaked into the Back Bay mansion she formerly shared with her ex-husband, bean magnate Benjamin Forster, of Forster's Beans, was found guilty Wednesday of fatally stabbing her 7-year-old son to death just 10 days after losing custody of him.

Jurors deliberated for less than two hours before finding Ann Forster, a 49-year-old woman with a history of mental illness and drug abuse, guilty of first-degree murder in the death of Maxwell Forster.

The charge carries a mandatory sentence of life in prison. Sentencing is scheduled for Feb. 16.

Investigators said Max was stabbed inside his bedroom of the 60-room, $14-million-dollar mansion while he slept the evening of Wednesday, May 14. The crime was not discovered until the following morning, when a member of the housekeeping staff discovered Ann Forster in bed with her child, "cradling him as if trying to soothe him to sleep." Emergency services were called, and the boy was pronounced dead shortly after 7 a.m.

Attorney Beck Alston said overwhelming evidence, including cellphone data, showed Forster killed her son, either for life insurance money, because of her mental health or after the stress of a custody battle with the boy's father.

Nora looked up, doing the math in her head. "I wonder if Miranda has any memory of that. She was just a toddler when it happened."

"Well, there's got to be something going on if the family has a bunch of therapists," Jason said with a shrug. "You know those families. The more fabulous their lifestyle, the more skeletons they have rattling around in their closets. I bet that's only scratching the surface of the problems they have."

"I wonder, though," Nora said as they drove off toward the crime scene. "The other two victims weren't rich. Maybe this has nothing to do with the other crimes at all. Maybe this was part of a botched kidnapping for ransom?"

He looked at her. "Maybe. But you heard her. She said the guy said he was going to kill her."

She blinked. No, she hadn't heard Miranda say anything of the sort. Likely, that had been while she was playing the nocturne in her head. "Okay," she said, looking over her GPS. "I've driven past this place, but I've never actually stopped. It's a dive. I thought it was closed. You really get your gas there?"

He nodded. "Every week."

"Okay. So lead the way."

CHAPTER SIX

As they drew closer, the Route Three Blackburn Gas-n-Sip didn't look any more reputable than Nora had originally thought on her many drives past it, heading to and from the field office. In fact, as she looked at the bars on the wall, the peeling advertisements for cigarettes, and the graffiti-covered walls, she thought it looked *worse*.

"It's amazing you've never been mugged at this place," Nora said as they pulled into the parking lot. The lot was usually empty, but now there were a few police cars and a K-9 squad parked there.

"Actually, I was." Snyder cut the engine. "Twice."

"You were?" she asked, scanning the area for the police officers. She didn't see them. They must've already gone into the woods.

He shrugged. "That was before I became an agent. I think the neighborhood's really cleaning up, though, since."

She stepped out of the car and noticed a man, slumped by the dumpster, a needle in his arm. "Right."

As they surveyed the area, looking for any sign of the officers, Nora imagined what it was like, as a scared former captive, rushing up the embankment and looking for help. She didn't have to strain herself. Miranda might have been used to tragedy, but it had to have been terrifying.

At this time of day, the traffic wasn't too bad yet. She started to jog across Route Three, headed for the shoulder, and Jason followed. He pointed into the woods. "There. I see one."

She strained and noticed a flash of blue. An officer with a German shepherd, making his way among the trees. Together, she and Jason made their way down the steep embankment and approached the officer, introducing themselves. The officer was Tom Vlasic, an old-timer on the force, a couple years from retirement. He seemed tired and out of breath.

"You find anything?" Nora asked.

He shook his head. "Been looking all day, too. I'm about beat. It's a swamp, and it goes all the way back. It's a lot of land to cover."

"How many guys you got out here?"

"Six. And some local guys are looking, too." He motioned them back to the squad car and laid out a map. "We took care of these two quadrants. But these two we still need to comb."

Snyder checked his watch. "We still have a good few hours of daylight. We'll give it a shot."

He nodded. "If you see anything, give me a holler. I'm going to go get Bootsy here watered."

Nora ruffled Bootsy's ears, and the dog licked her wrist. "Good girl. You're a good girl," she said to her, stooping to let the dog lick her face. She laughed.

As the officer took the dog away, Snyder looked at her. "You know, you never get that excited around humans."

She shrugged. "Dogs are perfect."

"And yet you don't have one." He scratched the side of his face.

"I wouldn't want my imperfect life rubbing off on a dog," she said simply, turning toward the woods. "Now how are we going to do this? Which way should we go?"

The agents decided to split up to cover more ground. The moment Nora entered the woods, she shuddered.

It happened every time she went into the woods now. A jolt of fear, a sickening déjà vu, but she could never quite call herself back to that moment. It was obvious she'd been running through the woods, though all she really remembered was the darkness. She'd had scratches from tree branches on her face, grass stains and mud on her knees. But that was all.

She took a few steps and heard her partner let out a low moan. "Dammit. I knew I shouldn't have worn my new shoes today."

The outburst broke the tension that had been pooling in her gut, and she let out a laugh. "You poor baby."

"Damn straight," he called back. "Spent a hundred bucks on them, and now I have mud in my socks."

She tramped through the woods some more, until the sound of her partner brushing through the forest disappeared, and the only thing she could hear was the soft hum of crickets and the chirping of birds. She looked around, trying to orient herself. With the heavy cover of branches overhead, it was nearly as dark as night.

As dark as it had been when she and Sophia had taken that shortcut from JP's. The brightest thing had been her sister's ponytail, swishing on her bare, tanned shoulders. *Come on. Move your slow butt. I don't want to be late. They're waiting for me.*

Nora was so lost in the memory, she didn't notice the exposed tree root until her foot had caught on it, and she went flying forward. She put her hands out, grabbing ahold of a small tree branch to prevent herself from getting a face full of mud. Sighing, she looked around and realized that she couldn't see the road from where she'd walked. Everything, in every direction, looked exactly the same.

That, too, reminded her of that day. Just a glimmer of déjà vu. Being lost. Though no one was chasing her now, the fear that struck deep in her heart was as arresting as it had been that day.

That was why she nearly jumped when a voice called her name. "Price!"

She clutched at her heart and realized it was only Jason. He wasn't visible, but she could tell the general direction from where his call had come. She took a step toward it as he shouted, "I found something."

She took off in a run toward the sound of her partner's voice.

*

The cabin didn't even look like a cabin at first.

Constructed of dark, pitted wood, it melded perfectly into the landscape of dark tree trunks, and was so covered in vegetation that it seemed to be in the process of being swallowed whole by the forest. The only thing Nora noticed, and just barely, was the white frame of a window, which was too straight and angular to have come from nature. As she drew closer, other things came into view—a rusting, broken-down generator, sinking into the ground at the side of the house, and a front porch, cluttered with stacks of rickety wooden milk crates.

Nora looked around. There was no path leading to this place, no driveway. No car, not even a bicycle. It was as if the person who lived here wanted to be cut off from the rest of the world.

She swallowed, forcing away those thoughts of déjà vu that threatened to intervene. Sometimes, when she tried to think of the place she'd been held, her mind conjured up images of a place like this. Or were they memories?

This place seemed familiar. Or maybe not. She couldn't quite tell.

Whatever it was, a deep, unsettling feeling fell over her, like a heavy chain around her neck, gradually pulling tighter.

Shaking that off, she walked around to the front of the cabin.

Jason stood at the front steps, hands on his hips, as if trying to decide whether to go in. Nora stepped through the knee-high grass in the front yard, past what looked like the remains of a broken soccer goal, and stood next to him. "Well?" she said, looking up at the front door. It might have been nice, once, as it had been painted red, the color of welcome. But now it was hanging off its hinges, and had multiple dings in the wood, as if an animal had been trying to claw its way in.

"Guess this is the place, huh?"

"I don't see any other creepy old cabin around here," she said, trying to make light of it, but her voice still trembled.

His voice was gentle. "You going to be—"

"I'll be fine," she said quickly, marching toward the front door to prove it. Climbing the three broken wooden steps, she made it onto the porch and took a deep breath, eyeing the open triangle of space in the upper left corner, where the door had separated from its frame. There, a single cobweb floated in the stagnant air, and all she could see beyond it was darkness.

She took a deep breath, sensing her partner's eyes on her back. He was just waiting for her to buckle under this pressure so he could come in and play hero.

As much as he loved that, lived for that, she wouldn't allow him it. She was a goddamn FBI agent, first in her class at Quantico. She might not have become numb, yet, to the trauma in her life, but she could sure as hell *pretend* to be.

She went to the door and shoved at it.

It creaked on the one remaining hinge, but didn't budge. She sensed it wasn't just stuck from disuse. There was something on the other side, wedged against it, holding it closed.

Interesting, she thought. If this was the empty cabin where Miranda Forster had been kept, she'd expected it to be abandoned, their suspect long gone.

But someone or something was clearly inside, and had barricaded himself within.

Nora turned back to Jason to question it, but by then, he'd already climbed the steps and she found him right beside her, a confused look on his face. He made a motion under his blazer for his gun, and she reached for hers out of instinct.

"Allow me," he murmured, then shoved up against the door. With one thrust, it instantly came off its hinges, falling into the room with a terrific crash that shook the floorboards beneath them.

Nora stepped inside first, even before the dust had settled. She'd been bracing herself for the sense of déjà vu to grow stronger, and it did. There was an old stone fireplace in the center of the room, with iron fireplace tools scattered around it. Other than that, most of the furniture was mismatched and old. The room smelled vaguely of pot smoke and mold.

“Price, look at this,” Jason said, poking at a latch among the dusty floorboards with the toe of his loafer.

Nora could vaguely make out the outline of the lid of a hatch. To the basement. The basement where …

Making her way to it, she sucked in a breath, remembering climbing a wooden ladder, the splinters pricking her hands, desperate for escape. Or was that just a dream? Had it really happened at all? Whatever it was, it made her stomach twist.

Then she looked up at Jason and nodded for him to open the hatch. It felt like the hardest thing she’d ever done, because as much as she wanted to see what was down there … she knew it would only make that unsettled feeling inside her grow worse.

As he reached for the rusted metal pull, there came a sound behind him. A simple shifting of floorboards, which probably happened all the time in a house as old as this one. But it was enough. Jason froze, and she peered past him, down a dark hallway, squinting to make out something in the black.

She only noticed the two eyes, glinting, when there came an otherworldly wail of anguish. Footsteps pounded like thunder, the floorboards creaking as if they were about to give way, and a giant wall of a man came crashing out of the darkness toward them.

CHAPTER SEVEN

Nora reached for her gun as the man lunged forward, landing on his knees between the agents. He was more scraggly salt-and-pepper hair than body, dressed in a ragged Baja hoodie and loose sweatpants. His eyes were wild, and his arms were flailing. The wail was replaced by an incoherent rambling, something about peace at the end of the world.

Nora watched him, her hand on her gun, still not removed from the holster. She exchanged an uncertain look with Jason, who'd already pulled his gun but looked about as confused as she was. The man didn't have a weapon, and wasn't appearing to attack *them*. He seemed a man possessed. Drugs, possibly. They'd certainly seen it before.

"Whoa, dude," Jason said, backing up to avoid a misplaced fist to the face. "Calm down."

The guy did nothing of the sort. As if he hadn't heard a word her partner was saying, the man suddenly jumped to his feet and took off through the open door.

At once, Nora took after him, pulling her gun from her holster and flying onto the porch, aiming at the man who was slowly lumbering away from them. "Freeze!" she shouted, but the man, in the throes of whatever trance he was in, continued, disappearing into the brush.

"Let's go!" Nora shouted, rushing after him. As if they were a well-oiled machine, she could feel Jason following, breaking to the left where she broke to the right. They'd tracked down a number of far faster fugitives this way, and soon narrowed in on the giant man, who seemed to be limping.

She was barely out of breath by the time she caught up with him. "Freeze!" she shouted again, but the man continued. "Hands up or I'll shoot!"

Charging past her, Jason launched himself on the man's back, but even that did not topple the enormous man at first. He staggered forward, straight into a tree, then spun, scrabbling at the agent's arms, which were clenched around his neck like a cape. Only when he had fallen to his knees did Jason break the stranglehold.

By then, Nora stood above him, gun drawn. When he looked up, red-faced, she pointed it between his eyes. "Don't even think about it."

Pouting, he fell back onto his enormous backside, breathing hard, and wiped at his nose. "I just want to be left alone."

"Sorry, buddy, but that's not going to happen," Jason said, giving him a shove.

Nora stared at him, trying to see his face in the sketch Miranda had provided. It was wrong—this man's face was round, his eyes beady, his hair full, oily curls. His forehead had three distinct wrinkles, from temple to temple, that hadn't been in the sketch. But that didn't mean anything, Nora assured herself. Sketches were notoriously, well, sketchy, and could be off by a mile.

But the fact still remained that this guy had stuck around. Why would any killer do that?

She decided not to concern herself with that. By then, a couple of officers who'd heard the commotion in the woods had arrived, and they took him into custody and walked him back toward the cabin.

Jason looked at her and opened his mouth to speak. She held up a finger.

"If you ask me if I'm okay one more time, I'm going to shoot you," she muttered, putting her gun back into its holster as they walked back to the cabin.

*

"I told you," the man said as he sat on the front steps of the cabin. "I didn't do nothing wrong. I just wanted to be left alone."

Nora paced among the weeds, her hands on her hips. They'd learned some things about their suspect. He was Tim Graff, an out-of-work carpenter from Worcester, who'd been making his way to Boston to find work. He'd admitted to smoking a little pot, but other than that, they'd run up against a brick wall. "This isn't your place, though. Your name isn't on the deed, is it?"

He sniffled, then brought both cuffed hands up to his face to wipe his nose. "Well, no. But it's empty most of the time. I didn't see no harm in it."

"Most of the time?" Jason asked.

He nodded. "Yeah, I been staying here a couple of weeks, ever since I lost my gig in Worcester. I go out, do some odd jobs when I can, come back here to sleep. But the other night, the lights were on. I had to sleep in the woods."

"The other night … you mean, two nights ago?"

He nodded.

Two nights ago. The night Miranda Forster escaped. Nora moved closer to him. "The lights were on? Did you happen to see who was there?"

He shrugged. "Yeah. It was a thin guy. Tall. He came out the door wearing like a jumpsuit. Like, all gray. For work."

"Like coveralls?"

"Yeah. That's it."

"He have a vehicle?"

"I didn't see one."

Jason murmured in her ear, "I saw a service road behind the house. Could've parked back there so you wouldn't see it from the front of the house. We can check for tire treads."

Not that that would help much, but it was something. She nodded. "Did you see his face?"

"No. He was wearing a mask."

Jason frowned. "A Halloween mask?"

"Yeah." The man shrugged. "Thought it was stupid, it not even being July yet. But whatever floats your boat, you know? That sure ain't the weirdest thing I've ever seen in these woods."

"Did you see anyone else? Was he with a girl?" Nora asked.

He shook his head. "I only looked for a second. Had to find a place to spend the night. I wound up camping in the woods."

"And when did you come back here?" Jason asked.

"Next morning. He was gone."

"Did he leave anything in the house?"

Tim Graff shook his head. "Nope. Didn't touch any of my stuff, either. Not that I had anything worth stealing."

They wound up staring at their suspect in silence, out of questions. Nora motioned Jason away from him and murmured, "What do you think?"

Jason glanced at him. "I think we can't keep him. He's just a squatter, and I don't think he's our guy. Do you?"

She shook her head. "No, he doesn't look anything like the sketch Miranda produced, either. But let's go take a look inside the cabin first."

They left the vagrant with the arresting officers and went inside, where a couple of other officers were already looking around the small cabin, making the main room excessively cramped. Someone was taking crime scene photos. They went down the hall and took inventory of Graff's things—his backpack full of clothes and blankets, his stash of food, his meager other belongings like a broken wristwatch and a camp stove. Then they went back to the hatch. It was open, and some of the officers were already inside.

Taking a deep breath, Nora didn't look at Jason as she climbed down.

When she reached the bottom of the small basement, her feet sunk into soft dirt. She looked around, her eyes landing immediately on a pipe in the corner. There was some thick, fraying rope wrapped around it, and black droplets which could've been dried blood among the dust. There were scratches on the ground there, as if someone had writhed and fought to escape.

This was the place.

Reaching out, Nora grabbed the cinderblock wall to steady herself as she noted the old table in the center of the room. It was bare, except for a thick, large butcher's knife.

At that moment, Nora felt as if all the air had been sucked out of the room. She couldn't say how much of this matched her own life. Maybe little of it. Maybe more. For all she knew, this could've been the place she and Sophia had been kept, all those years ago. It didn't matter, because it was enough. She gulped air, trying to pull it into her lungs, but couldn't find the breath. Bowing over, she started to hyperventilate.

Staring at the ground, she sensed all eyes in the room on her, even as the walls began to close in. Their voices echoed so she couldn't make them out. She could hear Jason saying something, calling her name, but she couldn't answer. Then there was an arm around her, pulling her up out of there.

As thankful as she was to be out, her cheeks burned with shame. She didn't want to be rescued. Not anymore. As soon as she could, she yanked herself from her partner's arms. "I told you, I'm fine."

He let out a short laugh. "Are you? Because that didn't look fine."

"I am fine. I just needed a moment," she said, turning away so he couldn't see the lie on her face. "This might've been the place where it happened, but the guy's long gone. Come on."

She started down the stairs in front of the cabin.

"Where are we going?" he called after her.

She turned. "Isn't it obvious? I think we only have one move right now."

He followed her. "Which is …?"

"I want to talk to Miranda Forster's coworkers at Mr. Creamy, " she said, marching through the woods. "She said she thought the guy was a customer. They had to have seen the creep that was stalking them, too, right? Or it could be on security footage."

CHAPTER EIGHT

Mr. Creamy was no place for a bean heiress.

That was Nora's first thought as they pulled up to the ice cream stand. It was one of those old-style buildings, circular in shape, with a giant dome on top, like an ice cream cone. There was a window in the front for customers to pick up their treats, and a small outdoor seating area with little red picnic tables. It would've been cute about fifty years ago, but now it simply looked old, like it had had better days. The cherry on top of the dome was a faded pink, and the paint all over the white building was peeling to a sad gray. The flickering neon sign in the window only said CRE, and most of the letters were missing from the board out front with all of the flavors.

Nora stepped out of the car into the wide parking lot, which the ice cream stand shared with a strip mall full of mostly abandoned stores. It looked like there'd been a bank there once, and a supermarket and a record store, but now they were only empty storefronts. Except for the two cars parked near the Mr. Creamy, there were a few cars parked in front of one open shop, a dollar store, far across the lot. Other than that, the place was empty. If Miranda had been working there alone that night, it would have been all too easy for someone to come up and grab her without being observed.

When she and Jason approached the outdoor window, she noticed two heads behind the counter. Beyond them, there was a family in the corner of the seating area, a mother with her two children, one in a stroller, the other a little boy of about four or five. The harried woman kept attempting to lick her vanilla cone while wiping the chocolate mustache from her rambunctious son's mouth and telling him to sit still.

A girl with a dark ponytail came to the window, smiling to reveal a mouth full of braces. "Can I help you?"

Nora reached into her pocket for her ID, but Jason spoke first. "Yeah, two cones. One vanilla, one chocolate. Rainbow sprinkles."

She looked at him as he reached for his wallet.

"What?" he said defensively, laying down a ten-dollar bill. "It's my treat."

She couldn't argue with that, though she did think that they'd look decidedly less professional eating ice cream cones with sprinkles while they asked the tough questions of the employees. But after her foray into the dungeon beneath the house, she could've definitely used the pick-me-up.

"Thanks," she said, taking the chocolate one from the woman and licking the top of it. Jason even knew her favorite ice cream order without asking her, which was a definite plus of working with him. As the woman handed over his change, Nora said, "Do you know Miranda Forster?"

The girl's brow lifted. "Are you police? I thought you were police."

Nora finally flashed her badge. "FBI."

The girl nodded. "I can't believe what happened. And right here, of all places. I never felt really safe here, and now I really don't. I keep checking over my shoulder, even though I know it's silly that anyone would come after me in broad daylight, like, right?"

"So you worked some shifts with Miranda? How long have you been working with her?" Nora asked.

"I've known her forever. She's actually my best friend. I feel so bad because, like, I got her this job, you know?"

"You did?" Jason asked, licking some vanilla from his knuckles. "You mind coming out and talking to us?"

She bit her lip, then nodded and stepped away from the counter, pulling the strap of her apron over her head. "Adam, hold the fort. I need to talk to these guys." A moment later, she appeared in front of the window, and the three of them wandered to a picnic table out front.

"What's your name?" Nora asked, stepping over the bench to sit at the table.

"Vanessa. Vanessa McClure." The girl was skinny, with ears full of piercings and perfectly manicured nails. "Have you seen her? Is she okay?"

"Yes, she's okay. She's in the hospital, recovering," Nora said.

"Oh, I'm so glad to hear that. I couldn't believe it when I heard she'd gone missing. I was so relieved when she was found. But I felt like it was my fault, you know? Getting kidnapped, right from here? My parents didn't want me to come into work today. But the police have been driving by, doing a loop every five minutes, so I feel safe."

"You're really close friends?"

She nodded. "Miri and I went to high school together. We were on the cheerleading squad, we joined the same clubs, we were in the same classes. So we became friends, even though I'm not a billionaire like her."

"This is public school?" Nora asked.

"Yep. Blackburn High. You'd never know she was from that fabulously wealthy family if you saw her on the street. Her parents were very big on making sure she kept it real. She had to earn an allowance. And they, like, wanted her to get a job to show she wasn't some spoiled brat. So I told her Mr. Creamy was hiring, and she got the job. We worked together after school, and this summer, and it was great."

She laced her fingers in front of her, nervously twiddling her thumbs, and Nora noticed a number of silver rings on her fingers. At first, she thought she saw a tattoo on her forearm, but then she realized it was probably just marker. The girl was young, like Miranda, after all.

"You worked together every day after school?" Jason asked.

"Not every day. I worked Tuesday, Wednesday, and Saturday, but Miri only worked on like, Wednesdays and Fridays, I think, and later, so she closed the store. She usually had to go to her therapy appointment first, downtown, right after school."

"Therapist?" Nora said, recalling the woman they'd run into in the hospital. "You mean Dr. Benson?"

The girl squinted. "No. She wasn't a doctor. Elle Squires. I think that was her name. Miranda liked her because she was young and fun and talking to her was like talking to a friend. At least, that's what she said." Vanessa giggled. "She was always talking about her therapist. Like, she wouldn't do a thing without asking for her advice. I guess that's a rich people thing. I mean, I know she had a couple of messed up things happen in her life, but really, she wouldn't do a thing without calling her. She was like, top of her contacts list, even before me."

Nora made a mental note of the name. "How long has she been seeing her?"

"At least since the beginning of the year. I think she had a couple before that, that didn't work out. But you're right. I think she was with the family doctor before then," she said with a smile. "I got the feeling she felt closer to Elle because she didn't have to worry about her, like, talking to her parents. You know?"

"She was keeping secrets from them?"

"No, I don't think so. She was a good person. I mean, she has a boyfriend they don't really like. And her father's really controlling, always checking up on her. I guess because of what happened to her half-brother. You heard about that, right?" When they nodded, her eyes went wide. "I can't blame him for wanting to keep an extra eye on her. I'm sure he's probably never going to let her out of his sight again, after this."

Jason polished off his cone, reached into his pocket, and flipped the pages of his notebook. "Can you tell us if there were any interesting visitors to the ice cream shop prior to Miranda's kidnapping?"

She nodded immediately. "Yeah, like, the police asked me the same question. There was a guy. He was a total creep."

On her phone, Nora pulled up the sketch from the description Miranda had given the police. She handed it to Vanessa, who made a face.

"Yeah, that looks about right. He was so weird. He'd just get his cone and sit in the corner, inside, and just stare at us." Her lips twisted. "I don't know if he came in on the Friday she was kidnapped, but it wouldn't surprise me. I wasn't working that day."

"Do you know if your employer has security cameras on the premises?" Nora said, looking around to see if she could spot one.

"Doubtful." She rolled her eyes. "The employers don't really care. Like, all they did was say they were going to install more lighting in the parking lot. Like, that will help? I told them I'm never going to be here after dark, that's for sure. I value my neck more than the minimum wage they're paying me."

Jason said, "Anyone here who might know who this guy is, then?"

She shook her head. "I'm just here with Adam, and he's new. He just started last week. Sorry."

Nora finished her cone and crumpled the napkin, then stood up and passed Vanessa one of her business cards. "If he does happen to come in again, can you give us a call? Thanks for your help."

The girl opened up her apron and slipped it over her head again. "No problem. If you do see Miri again, let her know I'm thinking about her. I've texted her, but … I guess maybe she doesn't have her phone?"

Nora nodded. "Sure, we will."

She and Jason went back to their car in silence. It was still early in the afternoon, before dinnertime, and yet the shadows of the old buildings cast an eerie and foreboding aura over the largely empty lot. Nora suppressed a shudder as she slipped into Jason's car.

"Where to, boss?" Jason said as he slid behind the steering wheel.

Nora opened her phone and looked down at the photo she'd snapped of the sketch. "Well, I think we should talk to Marjorie Hanson and Fawn Klasky. Maybe they've seen this guy."

He winced. "There's no other way?"

"Can you think of one?"

"No." He sighed. "I guess. Fine."

Truthfully, Nora would sooner have walked through a pit of rabid wolves. The two women shared a terrible bond—both were mothers to murdered girls. One, Nevaeh Hanson, an eighteen-year-old runaway whose body had been found three weeks ago in a creek bed; the other, Joy Klasky, who had disappeared sometime during her walk home from school. Nora and Jason had spent weeks on the two cases and had found no other similarities. Sure, both girls were young, from Blackburn County, and now, dead … but that was where the similarities ended. Nevaeh was a hellraiser, a troubled teen. Joy was a shy, mousy girl, a straight-A student at an all-girls prep school, who hung with an entirely different crowd. One had been strangled, the other stabbed to death. One showed signs of being sedated and bound, the other did not.

The thought of those girls tangled Nora's nerves. She'd had to endure months of questions from those mothers, asking whether they'd found the man … and had eventually had to endure the abject, heart-wrenching feeling of failure that came with telling the women that no, all leads had gone cold. The man had escaped.

Now, when they showed up on those mothers' doorsteps, of course, they'd expect news. Answers. Yet all she had was more questions.

And another murdered girl. The ultimate mark of their failure—another senseless slaughtering they'd been unable to prevent.

But if it would save someone else, she'd do it. "All right. Let's start with the Hansons first. Their house is closest."

He nodded and turned the car in the direction of the Blackburn County Trailer Park, and the mother of a murdered young girl.

CHAPTER NINE

Nora slammed the door to Jason's sedan and stared up at the modest ranch house belonging to Fawn Klasky. She took a deep breath, letting it slowly out.

Their attempts to find Marjorie Hanson had failed. Marjorie had been a single mother when her daughter disappeared, just scraping by while living in the only trailer park in Blackburn County. She'd had a hard life, filled with the usual—drugs, alcohol, a string of abusive partners. But Marjorie had gotten her life on track, trying to provide a good life for her teenage daughter. After Nevaeh had been found murdered, though, Marjorie had been so beside herself that Nora thought it only likely she'd take one route … right off the rails.

And apparently, she had. Her trailer had been abandoned, and neighbors said she'd just up and left in the middle of the night. One said he heard she'd gotten back into drugs.

Of course, Nora felt responsible. If only they'd found the killer, maybe they could've saved the last bits of Marjorie Hanson's sanity and prevented her from this catastrophic downfall.

Now, as she looked up at Fawn's house, she braced herself for more bad news.

Joy Klasky had had a more stable life than poor Nevaeh. Other than a car accident when she was a new driver at sixteen that had fractured her wrist, the girl had lived a relatively peaceful and trauma-free life. She'd grown up an only child in a modest, middle-class family, both parents still together, and they'd doted on her, sending her to expensive private schools to ensure she had the best education possible. After the murder, both parents had been understandably devastated, and it was Fawn who called Nora's office almost every day, asking for updates. Of course, as time went on, there was less and less information to give. Eventually, Nora had to tell her that while the case was still open, all leads had gone cold.

It had been over six weeks, and the only thing Nora had heard regarding the Klaskys was that Fawn and her husband were in the process of a divorce.

Yet another thing Nora blamed herself for—the destruction of a perfectly good marriage.

Jason stepped next to her and looked at the mailbox, which had the name KLASKY painted on it in black. "Well, at least it looks like she hasn't moved."

Nora called his attention to the FOR RENT sign in the window. "Yet."

"We should at least check it out," he told her, jogging up the steps and knocking.

Nora followed, noticing that the house wasn't as immaculate as it had been weeks ago, during their first visit. The lawn was overgrown, the flowerbeds full of weeds. The front porch could've used a good sweeping. Even the faded WELCOME mat, pushed to the side of the door, seemed to say, "Go away." By the time she reached the front door, it swung open, revealing only a shadow of the Fawn Klasky she'd once known.

Fawn's eyes were hard. "Agents," she said, looking between the two of them as she opened the screen door for them. "Do you have news?"

"Hello, Ms. Klasky," Nora said as she passed into the foyer. A single glance around, and she noted the disarray—plates piled in the kitchen sink, shades drawn to shut out the rest of the world, a musty smell that hadn't been there before. "Not on your case specifically. But there's been some developments in another case and we hope that might shed some light on yours."

"All right," she said, showing them into the dark living room. It was a formal room, and might have been elegant at one time, but now it just seemed unused and cold, with its dark-wood, uncomfortably stuffy Victorian furniture and wallpaper of brown, dead-looking flowers.

Nora sat on the edge of a velvet Queen Anne chair as Jason lowered himself onto the sofa surrounding a spindly, oval coffee table with a number of round water stains from cups that had been left there without a coaster. She looked up at Fawn Klasky, whose short, smart bob was now ragged. Her eyes were heavy and dark-circled, and she was thinner.

Just like Nora's mom, she was only a ghost of the woman she'd once been. And just like Nora, her nails were bitten to the quick.

Before either of the agents could speak, Mrs. Klasky said, "This is about that girl that was kidnapped, isn't it? I heard about it on the news. Do you think that whoever did that was responsible for my Joy?"

“We’re looking into that possibility,” Jason said, once again as gently as if handling a baby animal.

Nora reached into her pocket and pulled out her phone. “We have a sketch of a man who might be responsible. We wondered if you’d take a look at it. It might be someone you’d seen, prior to Joy’s disappearance.”

“Of course,” Fawn said, taking the phone and setting it in her lap as she stared at the sketch. Then she handed it back. “No. I’ve never seen that man.”

Nora had expected her to be unsure, at the very least. After all, she’d only looked at the sketch a moment. “Are you certain? Can you take a—”

“I’m very certain. I’d remember a man like that,” she said, pushing the phone back over to her. “I’ve never seen anyone like that in my life.”

Jason pressed his lips together. “All right. Did your daughter know Miranda Fa—”

“No. I’m sure of that, too.” Her brow wrinkled, suggesting disappointment, and then she let out a sigh. “You did this before. Trying to connect my Joy’s case to that runaway’s, despite having no evidence of that whatsoever. They didn’t know each other, they didn’t have anything in common. And you wasted time. My Joy’s killer got away. I’m no expert in crime, but I think you’re wasting time here, too, looking in the past.”

“That might be the case, but old sins cast long shadows, though,” Jason pointed out. “And we’re looking into every—”

“You’re wasting time looking here,” she said, standing so abruptly that her knees banged against the coffee table, shoving it aside on the oriental rug. “Now, if you’ll please …”

The woman trailed off, but Nora filled in the sentence: *Leave me in peace, to mourn the murder you weren’t able to solve, alone.*

Quietly, Nora stood, and with Jason, walked toward the exit. As she reached the doorway, she noticed a photograph on the table. It was of the smiling, though slightly awkward young Joy, standing next to a car, arms stretched as to show it off. Nora had never seen it before. She’d seen plenty of photos of the murdered girl in the file—graduation photos, prom photos, photos of birthday parties and Christmases from happier years—enough to haunt her forever. But this one was new.

Nora lifted it and tilted her head. “This photo. It must’ve been taken recently—”

Fawn Klasky all but snatched it from her grasp. “Yes. I don’t like it. That car … it was totaled shortly after the photo was taken.”

Jason filled in. “Oh, right. She was in a car accident, wasn’t she? Hurt her wrist?”

Fawn nodded. “Hurt more than just her wrist. A little boy in the other car got sent to the hospital. Oh, he’s fine now, but Joy felt so guilty. She didn’t want to drive again, which was why she was walking home that day …” She hugged herself tight. “Even the therapist couldn’t talk sense into her, that it wasn’t her fault.”

Jason let out a sympathetic “I see,” but something caught in Nora’s mind, a stone they hadn’t turned during the initial investigation. “Therapist?”

Fawn nodded. “She saw one. Or two. Only a few sessions, I believe. My husband handled most of that. But nothing really seemed to help, so she gave it up.”

And there it was. Miranda Forster had been to multiple therapists. Neveah Hanson had, too, all her life, to deal with her disruptive home life. Neither had ever found closure from the therapy they’d sought. And now … Joy Klasky. As perfect as her life was on the surface, she’d been seeking outside help for her issues, too. Why hadn’t they made that connection before?

Nora looked at Jason, wondering if he was thinking what she was thinking. His brow was raised, his expression the same as hers. “Do you happen to know the name of the therapists she saw?”

The woman shook her head. “Like I said, my husband … well, let’s see. There was one. Elle something. Elle …?”

“Squires?” Nora prompted, remembering the name that Vanessa had mentioned at Mr. Creamy.

Her dull eyes lit up. “Yes, that’s it. I remember her because she was younger. Less formal. I thought she might finally connect with Joy. But … well …”

Nora nodded. “I understand. Sometimes it is hard to find the right match,” she said. *Or in my case, impossible.*

When they stepped out onto the porch, Jason spoke first. “The therapist. Why didn’t we think of that before?”

“Because we’re idiots,” she muttered, so busy plugging the name Elle Squires into her internet search as she jogged down the steps that she practically body-slammed Jason’s car at the curb. “Here. I have an address for her office, only a few blocks from here. I wonder if Neveah Hanson saw her, too.”

"Guess there's an easy way to find out," Jason said, hurrying to slide into the driver's seat.

CHAPTER TEN

Nora was happy that it was after hours, and Elle Squires's office was closed for the day. She didn't think she could take another office with warm vanilla walls, ambient lighting, and comfy furniture that screamed, *Open up to me!* So she was practically ecstatic when she called Squires's after-hours number, and the cheery therapist suggested they stop by her apartment.

Unfortunately, as they looked around the living room, Nora realized she was not going to avoid the feeling of being psychoanalyzed at every turn. The room was full of those comfortable, homey touches that seemed so forced in Dr. Mathison's office—plants in terra cotta pots, cheery, bright paintings, and soft, overstuffed everything. There was no furniture, though, just bright throw pillows everywhere on the shag carpeting.

Sitting there, cross-legged on the rug, across from Jason, Nora frowned. "You think she owns a chair?" she whispered.

Jason looked just as unsettled as she was. "I don't know. I feel like I'm in a rumpus room for adults."

"Well … maybe it's a good thing. No furniture to break if one of them has a psychotic episode?"

He shook his head. "It's weird. *Fruity*. I don't buy this crap can help people."

Elle Squires returned from the kitchen, then, with a tray of tea and cookies. Despite them telling her they weren't interested, she'd insisted. The woman was overly happy, excited, and barely let them get a word in edgewise, which made Nora wonder how she conducted her sessions—did she ever just listen to her patients?

"Here we go!" the woman said, stepping barefoot onto the shag carpet. She was wearing a long, flowery cardigan, which made her look matronly, but underneath the thin fabric was a black catsuit covering a slight, wiry body. Her face looked like that of a young boy. Her eyes glimmered as she handed them each a teacup. "Yes, I know, it's odd not having furniture. But when I have my group sessions here, this deconstructed space is a lot more freeing for the participants. There are no preconceived notions, and there's no protocol as to who should sit where. They can let it all hang out, you know?"

Jason balanced his teacup uneasily on his knee as he looked around. "Sure," he said, his voice full of doubt. "So you have sessions here at your home?"

"Just a group session now and then. Personal appointments are in my office downtown." The woman curled up easily among the pillows, setting her teacup down gracefully in front of her. "Now, what is this about? You mentioned Miranda?"

Nora sipped her tea, which wasn't regular tea. It tasted bitter, like some odd spice she'd never had before. "Yes, you treat her, is that right? She mentioned—"

"As long as she mentioned it, yes. I wouldn't want to violate my patient confidentiality agreement."

"Of course," Nora said. "I'm sure you heard about the ordeal she went through."

Elle nodded. "The kidnapping. Yes. Terrible thing. After all the progress she's made. I'm sure she's a wreck. But thank goodness she escaped. She's a scrappy girl. A survivor."

"Definitely," Nora agreed. "And that's why we were hoping you could help."

"Of course. I'm happy to cooperate, though I'm not sure I'm going to be of much help. I was as shocked as everyone else when I found out what had happened."

"You also saw Joy Klasky this year," Jason pointed out.

Her brow wrinkled. "Who?"

"Joy Klasky. She'd been in a car accident?"

Elle shook her head, as if trying to loosen something from the deep recesses of her mind. "Oh, yes. Joy. She was afraid of driving. Poor thing."

It seemed odd to Nora that her own therapist wouldn't recall her, especially since she'd met a tragic end. "You don't remember her?"

"Well, I only saw her once. For a consultation. She determined it wasn't a good fit, I suppose, because she never booked another appointment."

"Or maybe it was because she was murdered?" Nora ventured.

Elle's smile faltered. "Murdered? What do you mean?"

Jason said, "Did you not read the story about the murdered girls in this county?"

"Well, I don't pay too much attention …" she said, taking a sip of her tea. "Of course, I knew Miranda. I met with her regularly, and her family's well-known. But Joy? Murdered? I didn't realize she was one of them. Oh dear. How terrible."

Nora stared at her, trying to determine if she was being sincere. She couldn't imagine anyone would hear the name and not put two and two together that she was one of their patients. "How many patients do you treat?"

"Oh, between my group meetings and personal appointments, I've seen hundreds," she said, running a finger along her teacup's rim. "I'm shocked. Shocked to my core. Poor girl. I don't even remember her very well. Just that she was shy, very shy. And scared. She didn't talk much."

With that, she looked up, and there were tears in her eyes. She reached over and plucked some tissues from one of the several dispensers situated around the room.

She dabbed at her eyes. "I'm so sorry."

Nora still wasn't quite sure what to make of this woman. She was odd, overly dramatic and emotional, but did that mean she was lying? Nora wasn't sure if she felt off about this woman just because she was a therapist, and Nora automatically was resentful toward therapists, or if it was something else. "You heard about the other murdered girl, then? Nevaeh Hudson?"

She sniffled. "Yes. Of course. That was terrible, too."

"She'd seen several therapists, too," Jason said, pulling her photograph of Nevaeh from his file and handing it over to her. "Does she ring a bell?"

Elle looked at it for a long time. "No. I haven't seen her."

"That photograph's old. When you saw her, she might've had a shaved head, a nose ring ..." he suggested. "She might have been referred to you by the local youth and family services branch. Do you work with family issues, runaways—"

Elle shook her head. "No, I don't. I don't take any referrals from them. Most of the people I work with are referred to me by their doctors. My specialized services aren't usually covered by insurance."

"Why is that?" Jason asked.

"Because, well, my therapies are largely experimental."

At that, Nora perked up. "Experimental therapies? Like what?"

"Oh, a bunch of things. I do various things, especially in my groups. They're on the cutting edge, and very exciting. Effective, too, at really dialing in on the hurt and getting a person to not just bury it, but accept their unique past and benefit from it. Of course, the tactics haven't gotten through all that regulatory red tape and nonsense yet. In time, maybe." Her eyes gleamed with excitement. "I'm honored to be at the forefront of what I think is going to be an incredible breakthrough in dealing with PTSD and other trauma."

Nora shifted in her seat. Her legs were getting pins and needles from the awkward way she was sitting. Jason asked more questions, but she barely followed. After Mathison, she'd all but given up on the possibility of finding someone to help her own situation. It seemed that every therapist promised something different, but in reality, they were all the same.

But Elle Spires had said all the right things. *A breakthrough in dealing with PTSD. A way to not just bury it, but to accept it, and benefit from it.*

Was that even possible?

She was broken from her thoughts when Jason put his teacup down in the saucer with an ungraceful clatter and tried to pull himself up to standing. "I think that's all we have," he said, gazing at Nora curiously. She had a feeling he'd been doing that a long time, trying to get her attention, while she'd been zoning out.

"Oh. Yes, that's all I have," Nora added, climbing to her feet as well.

As they walked to the door and said their goodbyes, Nora hesitated. Then she looked at Jason. "Why don't you go down and pull the car around? I just have a quick question for Ms. Spires," she said softly.

"Yeah?" he asked, a little confused. Something must have dawned on him, because he quickly said, "Oh, sure. I'll see you downstairs."

As he left, she closed the door and turned to the therapist. "Can I ask you a little bit about those experimental therapies?"

Elle smiled. "Is this professional curiosity, or personal?"

"Personal, mostly," she said, shifting from foot to foot. "I'm just interested in what it entails ..."

"Oh, well, my group sessions aren't like normal group therapy sessions. We engage in group accelerated resolution therapy, or ART, which is different from what you might have heard about ART in that it can produce results in only one session. The exercises have been incredibly effective, and yes, fulfilling for me, because it doesn't just let a person move on. It allows them to embrace the traumatic ordeal as something that made them into the wonderful person they are, to accept it."

Nora listened, rapt. "I'm sorry ... but how is that possible?"

She smiled mysteriously. "I suppose you'd have to see for yourself. Have you ever been to a group therapy session?"

Nora shook her head. "I assumed it was kind of like you see on television. People sitting in a circle, introducing themselves and sharing their sob stories."

Elle snickered. "Yes, I know. And then they all sit around and provide affirmation to each other, while enjoying bad coffee and stale donuts, before going home and wondering if it would be worth it to go back. Not at my session. In my sessions, people don't *need* to come back. Because they're cured."

Nora's mouth opened, and she found herself speechless for a long moment. "Cured?"

"I know. It sounds too good to be true. Believe me, that word—cured—is not one to be used lightly in my line of work. With PTSD, there's always a fear that trauma can resurface, pulling a patient deeper into that downward spiral. The slightest thing can trigger it. But my therapy eliminates all of those triggers … and the people who experience it lead remarkably fulfilling lives, with hardly any relapse."

Nora shook her head, trying to understand. It seemed too good to be true. "Was Miranda part of it?"

Elle shook her head. "Miranda never came to my group therapies. I suppose since I only met with Joy once, she never did, either. I can sense you have some trauma in your past?"

Nora nodded. "Something happened to me … and I don't remember a lot of it."

Elle reached out and squeezed Nora's forearm. "I understand. You're not alone. But the amazing thing about this therapy is that it can resurrect all those memories, but in a safer way, so that you're no longer tortured by them."

"That can't be …" Nora gasped, her voice barely a breath.

"It's possible." She held up a finger, then reached into the table in the entranceway and pulled out a small business card. "Here. Our next meeting is tomorrow night. Why don't you come by and see how it works. You don't have to participate. You can just observe."

Elle stared at the card, which said, *Elle Squires—Mind, Body, Spirit. Awaken a New, Stronger You.*

Nothing about therapy. Nothing about moving on. None of those trite buzzwords and cliché phrases used by every other therapist Nora had seen. No talk of medications or any of those things that hadn't worked for Nora in the past. This was something new.

And she was all about new. If there was a chance it could work and help her bring back memories of that night so she could finally find out what happened to Sophia… she was there.

Even if it wound up taking time away from the investigation at hand, if she could have answers to Sophia, it would be worth it in the end.

The only thing was, what would she tell Jason? From the look on his face, he hadn't bought any of what Elle Squires was selling. It had been written all over every one of his features—he'd thought this therapist was … what had he said? *Weird.*

"I'll think about it," she said, taking one last look around the "rumpus room for adults." It was a little weird, she had to give him that. But all of the normal things hadn't done squat for her. What would Jason think of her if she actually bought into it? "Thanks."

"Anytime, Agent," she said, moving to close the door. "I hope to see you here tomorrow night!"

Nora quickly ran down the stairs and out the front door of the apartment building, where Jason's car was idling by the curb. She'd already pocketed the card by the time she slid into the front passenger's seat.

"That was weird," he mumbled as she slammed the door. "And it didn't give us much to go on, if Nevaeh never saw her."

Nora nodded, staring out the front windshield absently. Her mind was whirling with things Elle Squires had said: *This therapy is that it can resurrect all those memories, but in a safer way, so that you're no longer tortured by them.*

It seemed too good to be true.

When she broke from her trance, Jason was staring at her. "So, where to, boss?"

She yawned and pointed across the street, toward the glowing red sign of a motel. They were on the other side of the county, far from home and headquarters, and too many thoughts were battling it out in her head—thoughts of Sophia, thoughts of the new case. She felt like they were all tangled together. "Let's stop in there. I need to get some sleep."

"Sleep?" He raised an eyebrow.

"Okay, okay. I just need to be still and think."

He nodded and did as she said, and she tried to push Elle Squires from her mind. She needed to untangle those thoughts and concentrate on the killer in their midst—not the ghost of one from over fifteen years ago.

CHAPTER ELEVEN

Nora sat with her back against the headboard of one of the two double beds in the hotel room. All the papers from all of the files were scattered among the sheets, illuminated by a single bulb from a lamp at her bedside. Canned laughter from an old sitcom rerun, as well as Jason's rhythmic snoring, provided the background noise as she pored over the files, the words jumbling together into an alphabet soup.

She blinked and looked up, then rubbed her eyes tiredly. Grabbing her phone, she checked it. Eleven p.m.

It was usually like this. She and Snyder, run ragged over a case, would stop in for "rest" at a motel. He would get plenty of it and wake up bright-eyed and bushy-tailed, ready to take on the world. The man could sleep through the apocalypse.

But Nora? Nora rarely slept, even in her own bed. And for good reason.

Too many ghosts.

Now, though, there was more. It wasn't just this newest development in the case of the Blackburn girls. It wasn't just this new information about the revolutionary PTSD treatment from Elle Squires. It felt like too much had happened, and now, she was missing something big.

She only realized that Jason had stopped snoring when he mumbled, his voice muffled by a pillow, "You gonna call it a night ever?"

She shook her head as she sifted through the papers. "That all three girls visited multiple therapists *has* to be a connection. It's rare, right? They're all so young."

Jason rolled flat onto his back. "Not in today's day and age. Seems like everyone and their mother has a therapist."

"Hmm. But that two of them had seen Squires? I wonder if we could be missing it, and Neveah Hudson did somehow cross paths with her. Maybe she just inquired into her services. That's something, right? I wonder who makes the appointments for her. I should go back and—"

"Whoa, whoa, whoa, hold on there, Tex," Jason said, pulling the pillow off his face and sitting up. He swung his long legs over the side of the bed, grabbed his phone, and looked at the time, wiping at his eyes. "You want to go back?"

"Well, I—"

The next time he spoke, he was completely awake. "What's going on here? I get the feeling it doesn't have to do with Miranda Forster or those Blackburn girls at all."

"No, that's not it. Of course, I'm focused on the case. I just feel like there's something there. There's a group meeting tomorrow, and she said anyone can just stop by—"

"Talk about a shitshow." When she didn't speak, he stared at her. "Okay … but going to a group meeting isn't going to get you in touch with the person who makes her personal appointments."

Nora shrugged. "All right, all right. She mentioned her group therapy was very effective."

"I'm sure they all do." He tilted his head. "Admit it. This isn't entirely about the Blackburn girls."

Nora looked away. "No. I guess not. And I know you think she's a quack. But you know me. I have to feel like I've covered every base. I just want to see what it's about."

"No, I get it. And you're right. I might think it's weird, but I think yoga and hot rock massages are weird, too. And people get a lot out of them. It's my fault. I'm easily weirded out."

She smiled.

"So yeah, you should go back. Hell, I can come with you. And while you're focusing on the healing, I'll see if there's anything tying these murders to their therapy. Okay?"

She nodded. "Maybe. Let me sleep on it."

He gave her a doubtful look as she piled up the papers and set them on the night table between them. "For real?"

"I'm going to give it a good try, at least," she said, turning off the light and sinking down under the covers. "Good night."

A moment later, comforted by the sound of her partner's snores, she fell fast asleep.

But almost immediately, she was jolted awake by the sound of her name being called.

Nora.

She looked up to find Sophia standing at the foot of her bed, giving her an exasperated look as she pulled her apron from around her slim waist. "Of course I should have the biggest share. You don't have to deal with those creeps leering at you. One of them tried to pinch my butt!"

Nora's heart wobbled in her chest. This had to be a dream. She knew it, of course. She'd had it plenty of times before. After all, she was sitting in a motel room. On the bed next to her, Jason snored softly. She was now an FBI agent, and a fully grown woman.

And yet, there was Sophia. That was why she felt like that fourteen-year-old girl again. She wanted to hug her sister tight, tell her how much she missed her. Jumping from her bed, she stopped when Sophia's eyes went over her head, to a clock that wasn't there. "Oh, I'm going to be so late! Come on! Hurry."

She went for the door, throwing it open and stepping outside, into the humid night air.

Nora ran for it, knowing what would happen next, but feeling somehow powerless to stop it. "Sophia! Wait! We shouldn't take the shortcu—"

She stopped when she reached the door and saw nothing but thick woods beyond the porch of the motel she and Jason had stopped at for the night. That hadn't been there before. Before, there'd been a parking lot full of cars. Now, the woods were so dark, like night, just like they'd been that day.

And Sophia was nowhere to be found. The leaves rustled, turning their pale undersides up in the wind, drowning out the sound of her footsteps.

A storm was coming. She could smell the rain in the air.

Nora knew the drill of this nightmare. She'd had it a thousand times. She stumbled out into the darkness, trees looming over her, misshapen and odd, like something in a funhouse mirror. Just when she thought she was making headway, everything would change, like the walls of a labyrinth. Thick mud would encase her feet, holding her still, or she'd sink into it, like quicksand. Every step forward would take her two steps back.

She cried out for her sister, begging her to go another way, and yet her voice made no sound.

Then she heard the scream.

Pulling herself through the mud, she launched herself into the woods, dodging sharp branches, roots, rocks, and other obstacles in her way. When she reached the clearing, she saw Sophia standing there, at the other end of it.

She looked perfectly fine, smiling, angelic, the Sophia everyone knew and loved. And yet the dread had already begun to pool in Nora's stomach. She knew what happened next.

Before she could open her mouth to warn her, big, paw-like hands reached out from behind Sophia, grabbing her. One clamped over her mouth, the other wrapped solidly around her waist. The last thing Nora saw was her sister's eyes, wide with terror, as she was pulled into the black.

She screamed and shot straight up in bed, to find Jason sitting on the edge of her bed, staring at her with concern. He didn't speak. He simply watched her as she let her heartbeat calm in her chest.

"Another one?" he asked after a moment, getting up to return to his bed.

She nodded and rolled over in her bed, away from him. "Yep. Another one."

CHAPTER TWELVE

Laura Porter smiled at her latest project. Though it had started off a little bumpy because she hadn't been able to get the hang of the new pattern, her crocheted amigurumi caterpillar was definitely starting to shape up. She'd already added the eyes and the mouth to the head, and now, the cutest little face smiled up at her.

She set her needle and yarn aside, looking up at her collection. She'd taken up crochet two years ago as a way to cope with the craziness in her life, and she had to admit, it had helped. Not only that, now she had a whole shelf full of cute little amigurumi creatures—a whale, a cat, a cow, a sheep, a butterfly … even a quite challenging octopus. Sometimes it was just a pleasure to look up at the shelf over the television set, not only because the animals were adorable, but because it was like a calendar, marking off how far she'd come.

Her eyes slipped toward the clock. It was after midnight! Funny how time went by when she was engrossed in a project. She hadn't even had dinner.

As if on cue, her stomach growled.

She patted it as if it were one of her pets. "All right, all right, let's get you something."

Taking her feet off the ottoman, she stood up, checking the floor as she made her way to the kitchen, though she didn't have to. She hadn't had animals to trip over ever since the incident. Of course, she couldn't trust herself to own *real* pets anymore, not with her history. But though she no longer had bunnies and cats and other furry things to get in her way, the stuffed ones provided a little bit of company.

She went outside to the back porch, where her garden had been putting out the most glorious beefsteak tomatoes all summer long. Grabbing two of the ripest, she went inside, sliced the tomatoes, toasted some bread, slathered it with mayo, and made herself a lovely tomato sandwich.

Setting the table for one, she sighed. Those empty spots made her heart ache, just as much as the quiet of the empty house. It hadn't used to be that way. All her life, she'd had a full house.

And then there was that night, two years ago, when everything changed.

The police called it a home invasion. She'd been sitting up late, dozing off in front of the television, her dog Blackie on her lap, when they'd come in, wearing all black from their ski masks to their combat boots. They'd waved a knife in front of her face. Scared to death, she'd told them to take anything they wanted, but to spare her dogs, Blackie and Martha, and those asleep upstairs—her husband and her two children. As they tied her up, she'd begged for mercy before they knocked her out.

But they did not give it to her.

Sometime later, she'd woken to the sound of the fire alarm, screeching overhead. In the haze and smoke, she saw the bodies of her dogs, lying on the ground, dead. The fire was everywhere, and it was all she could do to escape with her own life.

When the fire department put out the flames, the house had been reduced to ashes, and everything Laura cared about had disappeared with it.

But she'd made remarkable strides in those two years. She'd gotten the help she needed, gotten a new place, a new job, a new life in this small town outside of Boston. She was, for the first time since the incident, content. Not happy, but at peace.

She'd just sat down to eat her sandwich when a realization hit her.

You didn't lock the door!

She rocketed to her feet, and then stopped and laughed to herself. She'd blamed herself for so long, for being the one to not lock the door that night, allowing the invaders easy access to her home. Since then, she checked the front door obsessively to make sure there was no way in. Sometimes, she'd go back five, six, seven times in a row, just to be sure every lock was twisted tight.

But she'd been so excited about her sandwich, she hadn't even thought about it.

I guess I am getting better, she thought with a smile as she hurried to lock the door.

She twisted the lock, shut the door tight, then typed her code into the keypad, arming her security system for the night. *There. Safe and sound.*

Then she turned around to her sandwich. A nice bedtime snack.

I should have milk, too. That always hits the spot before bed.

She was about to head for the kitchen when she noticed the dirt on the hardwood floor.

No, not simply dirt. Big, dirty footprints, heading into the kitchen.

She inhaled sharply and froze. Her eyes went to the door. *Escape. You have to escape.*

But before she could, a figure in black clothes and a ghastly Halloween mask stepped out of the shadows and advanced upon her. She didn't even have time to scream.

CHAPTER THIRTEEN

When Nora woke up, she felt like she'd been lying in the middle of a highway at rush hour all night. Everything hurt, from her head to her feet. Slowly and clumsily, she made her way to the bathroom in her pantsuit and went to brush her teeth.

As she was brushing, she caught sight of Jason sitting at the table by the window. He had gone out early to get two coffees and was now scanning the files. He looked as ready as he always did in the mornings. It made her groan. "Can you maybe not be such a morning person?" she muttered to him, taking the coffee from him.

"I figure that's my job as your partner. To be the yin to your yang," he said, packing up the file. "You ready?"

She yawned, then hitched her bag over her shoulder. "Guess we might as well head out. Where we off to?"

"I thought we should check the area around that cabin. Someone might have seen something."

"I thought it said in the file that the police interviewed the cashier at the Gas-n-Sip, and he didn't see anything," Nora said.

"Yeah, but look at this," he said, setting down his coffee and opening up the map that the police had used to find the cabin. He pointed to a spot. "That's where the cabin was found. And though she might have run this way"—he pointed toward the location of the Gas-n-Sip—"this is closer."

She squinted. There was a strip mall in the other direction. Which actually made sense. They'd come to the cabin from the back. But the driveway had been at the front of the house. There was a far better chance that someone on the other side of the forest would've seen the culprit. "Damn. I'm an idiot. You're right."

He grinned as he folded the map. "Don't worry. Never have held it against you."

She went to elbow him as her phone started to ring. She looked at the display. "Durham," she whispered, bringing the phone to her ear. He was probably looking for an update, not that they had much of one. "Hey, boss."

"Price," he said shortly. "There's another one."

Nora Price's heart froze in her chest.

*

An hour later, the two FBI agents arrived at the scene of the crime.

While it was still Blackburn County, it was on the other edge of its boundaries, through the traffic of the morning rush. The neighborhood was called Hunter's Meadow, and it was a small, wooded enclave with tiny 1950s-style homes, all identical, painted various pastel shades. The victim's house was a pale yellow, and despite its age, showed pride of ownership. The flowerbeds were neatly maintained and filled with black-eyed Susans and geraniums of all colors. There were hanging flowerpots spilling with purple petunias, and there was a large wooden sign that said WELCOME propped up beside the door.

Nora walked past the police cars choking the street in front of the house, and noted the rosary hanging from the rearview mirror of the small, white compact car in the driveway.

"Agents," the mustached, older police officer said, shaking their hands. "They told me you were coming over. I'm Officer Marsh. Topham's a small town. We've never had anything like this here."

"I understand," Nora said quickly. That was the same thing most rural, inexperienced PDs said, and she was eager to get to the nuts and bolts of the investigation. "Can you tell me about the victim?"

He handed her a folder. "Laura Porter. Thirty-six."

She opened it, paging through, looking for a photo of the woman. There wasn't one. "Thirty-six?"

"That's right, she lived here alone," he said, leading them down a narrow path to the back of the house. There was a deck there, with a garden bursting with ripe produce, including tomatoes and cucumbers. The smell of fresh basil hung in the air as he pointed to the back door, allowing them to take a look inside.

"Alone?" she asked, peering in. The owner of this house appeared to be a mature, domestic type, who enjoyed not only gardening, but her crafts, as well. There were various needlepoint works on the wall, and an entire shelf of what looked like crocheted animals. But the thing that immediately drew their attention was the sight of some dirty footprints and the shards of what might have been a broken vase on the floor between the living area and the kitchen. Mingling with the mess were what looked suspiciously like drops of blood.

"Well, yes, except for her amigurumi," the officer said as she stepped in, looking at the kitchen table. There, on a single place setting, was a plate with an uneaten sandwich.

Nora frowned. "Ama-what?"

He pointed to the shelf. "Those animals. That's what they're called. It's Japanese."

"Oh." She exchanged a look with Jason, who looked similarly troubled. It wasn't their perpetrator's norm to take an older woman, but then again, considering how much he varied his modus operandi, the perpetrator didn't seem to have much of a norm. It was within Blackburn County, which meant it still could've been the work of their man. Then she retraced her steps and checked the door, and the rather complex security system on the wall. "No sign of forced entry?"

"No, seems she might have let him in? So we figure it might have been someone she knew."

"Reasonable assumption," Jason said with a nod as he looked around. "Unless she just didn't lock the door. Pretty safe neighborhood, right? Bet they usually have their guard down around here. You find any prints?"

He shook his head. "Just the victim's."

"Anything missing?" Jason asked.

"No. Her purse was found right on the sofa, there, in the entrance, and she had a hundred bucks inside." He motioned to a velvet sectional in the living room. "No license, but apparently she doesn't drive."

"Who reported it?" Nora asked as they left the house and went out to the front yard. The street had nice, mature trees, but the homes were small bungalows, almost on top of one another. "Neighbors this close, someone must've seen something."

"No. So far, none of the neighbors even heard so much as a peep. It was a coworker. Laura didn't show up to work this morning—she works at the pharmacy on the corner—and so her friend came to check on her and found the back door open, and Laura Porter nowhere to be found. The coworker, Tammy Reynolds, called us right away."

Nora scanned the sleepy neighborhood street, made into a bit of a circus by the presence of all the cop cars and the many uniformed officers. Neighbors were standing on their porches, watching curiously, but staying a respectful distance away from the fray. There was a middle-aged woman leaning against an SUV and smoking a cigarette as she spoke to an officer. She looked frazzled. "Is that her?"

He nodded and motioned her forward. "Hey, Bill," he said to the questioning officer. "These are the FBI agents I told you about. I'm sure they're going to have questions for Ms. Reynolds."

Bill stepped away, and Tammy Reynolds stubbed out her cigarette on the curb with the heel of her boot. "How long's this going to take? I left a trainee in charge of the register at my work."

"Not long," Nora assured her. "You two have been working together a long time?"

"For the past year and a half. I'm the manager at the Care-All. She's one of my best workers, and we've gotten pretty friendly, too."

"Do you know of anyone who would want to hurt her?"

Tammy shook her head. "Who'd want to hurt her? She was quiet, sweet, did her work and went home. She wasn't bothering anyone. And she was nice to everyone. I don't think she had a mean bone in her body. I've never even seen her get upset. Not once."

"And when was the last time you spoke to her?" Jason asked.

"Last night. We worked the afternoon shift together, and I said goodbye to her and she went to her car."

"Did she mention whether she was going to do anything last night?" Nora asked. "Anyone she was going to see, a date or appointment or something?"

Tammy dug her hands into the pockets of her sweatpants and chuckled. "She said she had a new crochet pattern she couldn't wait to tackle. That was about as wild as Laura's nights got these days."

"A single woman like her? She wasn't dating anyone?" Jason asked.

Tammy's face went dark. "Oh, god, no. Not her. Not with her history."

Nora looked at Jason, who shrugged. "What history is that?"

The woman pulled a pack of cigarettes from her pocket and tapped one out, placing one between her lips, and mumbled, "No one told you?"

They shook their heads.

Nora assumed she'd say something about a domestic abuse incident, or a string of cheating lovers. Clearly, the two women were close, and had shared their sordid pasts. But what Tammy said next caused both hardened agents to wince. "Two years ago, she was the victim of a home invasion, and her entire family was murdered."

"No kidding … Jesus," Jason said absently, then snapped his fingers. "Yeah … I seem to remember that. They ransacked the house and burned it to the ground with the residents inside. She was the only one to escape. That was the saddest story I read in a long time. They caught the thugs, didn't they?"

Tammy nodded. "A bunch of teens. They're in prison, as far as I know."

Whenever Nora heard about people going through traumatic experiences, she never felt solidarity with them. She always simply wondered why they all seemed to be getting by so much better than she was. Maybe Laura Porter had gotten where Miranda had gotten—she was numb.

There was the possibility that this kidnapping was related to that event … but then again, sometimes, people were just unlucky. "Well, then," she said to Jason, "forget your theory about her probably leaving the door open at night. She'd have been too scared to do that."

Jason nodded, and Tammy said, "Oh, she was maniacal about that. Whenever we closed up? She sometimes checked the lock on the front of the store five, six times. I joked with her and called it an OCD tic. But she knew it was a problem and she said she was getting help for it."

"Help for it?" Nora repeated, her excitement growing. "You mean, like from a therapist?"

She nodded, and Nora and Jason exchanged a look.

"Do you know her therapist's name?" Nora asked.

She shook her head. "Someone downtown. But I don't know the name."

Nora made a mental note of it and turned to go back into the house. If her hunch was correct, maybe this was the connection they were looking for.

CHAPTER FOURTEEN

Nora pulled another page down from the wall calendar that was hanging from the door of the kitchen pantry. She'd gone all the way back to March and was starting to notice a theme. "This is getting a little ridiculous."

"You want to talk about ridiculous?" Jason asked, looking over the items on the kitchen counter. It was cluttered with everything from tape to pens to drink cups to medicine bottles. He was busy taking photographs of the many different bottle labels. "There isn't a single photograph of her or her family in this house. But there's enough medication here to kill a horse. Some of them I've never heard of."

"Makes sense, if there was a fire in her house. Maybe she doesn't have any," Nora muttered, deep in thought. "Dr. Landon. Dr. Michaels. John Aspen, Certified Hypnotist… Look. She's had a bunch of therapy appointments. She taped the business card with the appointment date to the calendar."

He glanced at it. "Makes sense. All these medications were prescribed by different psychiatrists. The woman was on some pretty heavy stuff. Oh, and crap." He held up a sleeve. "It's not all for her brain. This is insulin. She diabetic?"

Nora shrugged. "We should probably check with the Blackburn County hospital and figure that out." She flipped to February. "And here's another appointment. With Dr. Benson. Why does that name sound familiar?"

"She was the woman we met at the hospital. The Forsters' therapist," Jason pointed out, now standing next to her. "So that's a connection. Any mention of Elle Squires?"

She sighed. "Who knows? Not that I can see. It's clear, though, that all of these victims have had some kind of past trauma, and were seeking therapy for it. It could be just a coincidence, but right now, it's the only possible link we have to show that our suspect's not just targeting random women."

Jason nodded as his eyes swept over the single photograph taped to the refrigerator. It was one of those studio photos with the smudged gray background, showing a smiling family: A pretty young mother, with her husband and two children. "Hell of a thing to happen to her. I don't blame her for wanting therapy. I don't think many people could survive a thing like that."

Nora nodded and looked at the photograph of Laura Porter, a woman she had never met. Nora had to agree with Jason; she didn't know what she'd do, either. She'd only lost one member of her family, and had her parents to lean on. But what would it be like to lose everyone? Not everyone could harden themselves to the trauma and make their way through life, numb. Some tragedies, no amount of therapy could fix.

"You remember reading about it? I don't," she said, though Nora had a good idea why. A couple of therapists along the line had suggested that she shut off the news. They'd said that sometimes, being fed depressing stories all day long could only exacerbate her condition, especially since she got enough of that working with the FBI. So she often ignored the news.

Jason nodded. "It was a hell of a thing. Her kids were only toddlers, and she was a homemaker. The neighborhood she lived in was one of the safest in Blackburn, so it got people pretty worked up. The thugs that did it were part of a gang, and it was some sort of initiation ritual. Really sad."

Nora flipped the pages of the calendar, noting more therapist business cards. It seemed like every therapist from Boston to Blackburn County was included. No Elle Squires, though.

"Hey, you know," Jason said suddenly, which made her look up. He was staring at her curiously. It looked as if there was something he wanted to say, but was debating whether to say it, which concerned her. The two of them weren't just partners … they were friends. She told him about his bad breath, and he harped on her whenever he thought she was gaining too much weight. They could say anything to one another.

But this? Clearly, this was something he couldn't—or didn't want to—say.

"What?" she prompted, hands on hips. "Spit it out."

"All these victims, seeing multiple therapists for their trauma. It just …" He rubbed the back of his neck. "Reminds me of someone."

She tilted her head. "Me?"

He nodded. "Well, yeah."

She squinted. "So what are you saying? That I'm the killer's ultimate target, and these other women are just to get my attention?"

Jason shook his head slowly, then shrugged. "No, I'm just making the connection."

She let the calendar fall back to the current month and exhaled slowly. "To tell you the truth, I've been thinking about how this relates to my life, too. Not like that, though. When we went into the place Miranda was being held … I …"

A scene flashed in front of her, those dingy cinderblock walls, the cold dirt floor, the rusting pipes … it made her shudder.

Jason noticed and stepped closer, looking into her eyes. "I thought something was up with you when we went to that cabin. You had a sense of déjà vu from that place?"

She let out a sour laugh. "Maybe. I don't know. You don't know how annoying it is to go into those places and wonder—maybe I'm having this feeling simply because there are similarities. Or maybe this is the *exact place* where it happened. It's like everything is there, but there's a veil over it, and I can't make out anything with certainty. Nothing is distinct."

He frowned. "Wait. You're saying that if it could be the exact place where you and your sister were held … you think *this* killer might be the same one who kidnapped you?"

She shrugged. "It's possible. Isn't it? So much is the same."

"But almost fifteen years have passed."

She closed the pantry door and said, "But you know as well as I know that stranger things have happened. There is a chance. And so part of me thinks that if I can pull more from my old case, we might actually find this guy."

He stared at her. She couldn't tell from his expression if he thought she was a wack job. Of all the people she knew, she respected Jason Snyder's opinion the most, but he leaked nothing.

That is, until he said, "I guess it's possible. But you shouldn't strain yourself. What we need to do is concentrate on the here and now. And that means finding Laura Porter before it's too late."

He made it sound so easy. "I'd love to do that. But where do we even start? We can go back to Benson and see if she has any ideas, since she saw two of the victims, but—"

He pointed out to the back of the house. "Look out there."

She followed his outstretched finger and saw nothing but green. A forest of trees upon trees. "What am I looking at? Nature?"

"Yeah. But what's in front of it?"

"A neighborhood …" she muttered, getting tired of this guessing game and wishing he'd just get to the point.

"Right. With a hundred neighbors, all of them practically eating, sleeping, and breathing right on top of one another."

"And?"

"And no one saw or heard anything? Even if he knocked this woman out so she didn't make a sound, he'd still have to drag her to the front of the house to put her in his vehicle. Someone should've noticed. Unless …" He smiled.

Now she was understanding where he was coming from. She looked out at the forest in the back of the house. Then she opened the door and stepped into the small yard. A person could cross the yard and wind up in the forest in fewer than twenty paces. Yes, Jason had a point. If someone was going to come in this back door, it would be a feat to bring the kidnapped person out the front of the house unnoticed. It'd make much more sense to escape into the tree cover.

She headed out into the trees, taking a few paces before she noticed, up ahead, a gravel road. It didn't look heavily traveled, but there were ruts and indentations where tires and feet had traveled. "Okay, okay," she said, more to herself than to him as she climbed up the embankment to the road's surface and looked around. There was nothing there, no sign of struggle, no evidence, but it seemed like the most viable way.

"You think he parked here? Yes, I think you might be right," she said, reading a sign attached to a tree, half-covered in vines. It said, *WARNING POTENTIALLY HAZARDOUS ROAD CONDITIONS AHEAD! LOGGING OPERATIONS ONGOING 24 HOURS. USE AT YOUR OWN RISK.*

Jason walked along the road for a short distance before turning around. "I think this guy's afraid of being seen. All the kidnappings have happened along rural or empty roads like this one. Think about it. The woods are right next to Mr. Creamy, where Miranda was taken from. In fact, you could use rural roads straight from there to the cabin. I think he's been getting around by using these logging roads, and if so, there's a good chance that some of the loggers who use these roads for work might have seen him."

She nodded. "Sounds like a reasonable assumption. Worth putting some eyes on," she admitted, though she wasn't sure she wanted to be the one putting the eyes on it.

"But …?" he prompted, squinting at her. Of course, he sensed her reluctance. "Don't you want to travel the scenic rural logging byways with me?"

She shook her head. “I think it’s more important that we figure out what we’re dealing with as far as Laura Porter’s medical history. Can you drop me off at the hospital? I can check around and ask into her psychiatric history, too.”

“You want to split up? Sounds like you don’t love me anymore.” He smirked.

She chuckled. “Sorry. But with Laura Porter’s medical condition, I think we’re in a race against time,” she said as they hurried back toward the house.

CHAPTER FIFTEEN

Jason Snyder didn't like being without his partner.

It wasn't that he was a follower. In fact, he'd been captain of his college football team. Leader of his regiment in the Navy. He'd always been one to take charge.

But when it came to Nora Price, they worked so well together, sometimes he felt like they were two halves of the same body. They complemented each other so well; she was always picking up things he missed, and vice versa.

So as he drove deeper down the logging road, constantly looking upward and expecting a giant tree to crash down on the hood of his sedan, he had the creeping feeling that he was missing something. The thick trees made the place midnight-dark and eerie, and it was so quiet, with his only company the occasional firefly sparking in front of him.

From the maps he'd checked, this work location appeared to be the closest to all three kidnappings. In fact, it was practically in the middle of three sites. If Blackburn County was a wheel, the kidnapping locales occurred on the outer edges of the wheel, and this site was in the very center. The cabin Miranda had been kept in was off one of those roads. Not only that, there were rural roads leading to each one of the kidnapping sites from this worksite. It only made sense that the suspect had used them to commit his crimes.

At least, it had sounded like a good idea at the time.

Now, he was losing confidence in his theory by the minute. These woods were vast. And he'd been driving for half an hour, swerving down unnamed streets that all looked exactly the same. He'd gotten all turned around and had no idea if he'd even find his way out, much less anyone who'd seen anything relating to the crime.

I bet this turns up a whole lot of nothing. I should've probably just gone with Nora, he thought.

It was not just because he thought he was at his best, as an FBI agent, when he was with her. The truth was, he worried about her. She was like the little sister he'd never had. She'd always been a little unpredictable and wobbly. Other agents asked how he could stand it, but he'd never minded.

But he couldn't deny that ever since they'd taken on this case, she'd gotten … well, worse.

There were times when she'd stare out into space, so far away, he had no idea where she could be. Or when she'd jump, suddenly, at the mention or sight of something that would've been innocuous to some people. He'd never forget the time a witness in another case, an old banker, had pulled out a pocket watch from his coat. Nora had all but gone ballistic. She'd begun hyperventilating, and he thought she might pass out. It was always something like that, keeping him on his toes.

But yesterday, in the cabin, she'd definitely been upset. And now, he knew it was with good reason—she thought she might have been standing in the same place she and her sister had been imprisoned, all those years ago. It had to be hell not to remember, to go through life not knowing anything for sure. After all, any man she met or interacted with *could've* been the man who'd destroyed her family.

He'd had a pretty vanilla life, so far. No trauma, even while in the Navy. He'd never seen any action at all. So although he'd never had to test himself, he was pretty certain he wouldn't have been able to go through what Nora Price had endured. And yet here she was, giving her all, putting bad guys away like nobody's business. He respected the hell out of that.

Snyder slowed to a stop when he saw another sign for the logging company. Up ahead, a clearing. He powered down the window and heard the faraway buzzing of electric saws.

He patted the dashboard of his car. His baby. It wasn't much, but it was the first car he almost owned outright. He only had two payments left, and couldn't wait until it was all his.

It'd be just his luck if a tree bashed its roof in.

So, leaving the car, he grabbed his phone from the cup holder, pocketed it, and headed up the road on foot.

As he walked, he thought more about Nora. The first time he'd met her, he hadn't thought much about her. They'd been partnered up almost from when they got to the academy, and at first, he'd regretted it. Most of the people in their class looked the part. Tall, strong, athletic, substantial. But Nora was skinny and a little awkward looking, with her hair in two braids—she looked like a schoolgirl, like a stiff wind would blow her over.

Jason Snyder, too, wasn't much to look at. He wasn't short, but he wasn't nearly as big and brawny as the other men in the class. They dwarfed him. He'd never been the greatest of athletes, but he held his own, dabbling a little in every sport. He'd felt like the last kid picked in gym when the instructor paired him up with Nora. All the other agents had laughed at them, thinking they'd come in dead last.

But they hadn't.

In fact, they'd worked better than anyone. Together, they'd worked smarter, not harder, making up for their lack of brawn with brains. By graduation, he was second in his class, and she was first.

He smiled a little at the thought, a smile that soon disappeared when he realized that Nora was going back to the hospital.

The same hospital where she'd *clearly* been on edge while interviewing Miranda Forster. Something had definitely been wrong. He'd seen it. But whether it had to do with Miranda or the hospital itself, he didn't ask. He only hoped she'd pull it together and get the information they needed.

The buzzing got louder and louder until it was practically earsplitting. When he reached the edge of the clearing, he saw the logging trucks, and the men working to clear the forest. A man in a hardhat and safety glasses stood at a barrier at the end of the road, blocking any traffic that came that way. He held up both hands, in heavy gloves.

"Whoa. The road is closed. You shouldn't be back here," he called over the noise.

Snyder flashed his credentials, and the man quickly came forward, over the barrier, and removed the plugs from his ears.

"Something I can help you with, Agent? Why're you all the way out here?"

"I'm looking into a case," Snyder said, scanning the area. A good chunk of trees had been clear-cut, almost as far as he could see down the road. "How long have you been clearing out here?"

"Six months. Putting in that new highway. That's progress, you know, huh?" he said, slapping Snyder on the back.

Snyder lurched forward, not expecting the contact. "Yeah. Sure. Have you personally been working on this site?"

He nodded, removed a glove, and extended his hand. "I'm one of the foremen on the project, sure. Name's Chuck Gravener."

Snyder shook it. "Hey, Chuck. So, you've been stationed right here most of the time?"

"Nah. I'm all over. There are a couple of different entrances to the site, and you can usually find me near one of them. It's a pretty big one, this site. Over a thousand acres right now."

"But you know these rural roads pretty well, then, if you've been working near them awhile?"

He scratched the graying stubble on his chin. "Oh, sure, better than anyone. Yeah, a lot of people say it's like a maze back here, with no road names or a street map, but I can probably find my way through it in the dark."

"Then you're just the man I'm looking for," Snyder said with a grin.

"If you're looking for the way back to the highway, just keep making lefts, and eventually you'll get there. That's what I tell everyone who gets lost around here."

"No, I'm actually looking for someone in particular." His eyes narrowed. "You see a lot of people who get lost in here?"

"Maybe one a day. Who're you looking for?"

"I don't have much to go on." He pulled out the sketch Miranda had provided. "Ever see this man?"

He shook his head. "No. Don't think so. There are a lot of weird-looking, weird-acting people around these woods, though," he said with a shrug. "I guess they're that way because they don't like people and they want to be left alone. But I've never seen that kind of weird."

"What have you seen? People doing weird things?" Jason crossed his arms, interested.

"Oh, yeah. Saw a couple of naked old people, getting it on in the woods, once," he said with a sly grin.

"And … anything else?"

"Just a bunch of hillbilly types, looking all suspicious, like they up to no good, you know? Probably are up to no good, considering. Usually they're dumping trash illegally or cooking up drugs or something like that. That what you're looking for?"

He shook his head. Snyder wasn't about to go door to door around these woods, looking for suspicious types. That could take the better part of his lifetime. "No … looking more for a man that might be kidnapping women. You see anyone like that? Might have a woman in the front seat that looked asleep, or like she didn't want to be there?"

Chuck shook his head. "No, nothing like that …" His face scrunched up as he thought. "Wait. You know, let me see that sketch again?"

Snyder unfolded the paper.

"Hey, you know, that could be someone I know. His name's Rupert. Bo Rupert. He's kind of a weird guy, real backwoods, two-toothed hick. Used to own a small parts shop in the middle of the woods, but lately, he barely goes out. Doesn't like people. From what I hear, he has a police record—when he was younger, he used to stalk girls around town. I used to see his truck on the road now and then, leaving his place. But I haven't seen him in a while. Could be him."

It was worth checking out.

"Can you give me his address?" Snyder asked, pulling out his phone to take notes.

"Sorry, people out here don't have addresses. He lives on one of these roads with no names. But I can point it out to you on a map, if you got one."

Snyder opened his phone to the maps section, hoping and praying that his phone would have some reception. When he finally pulled it up, Chuck looked at it and pointed to a location. "Right there. You're going to have to make rights instead of lefts, from here, to get there. And it might get you lost, just saying. He's pretty deep in the middle of nowhere."

Jason Snyder winced. He'd thought *this* was in the middle of nowhere.

"Thanks," he said, heading back to his car with his phone still in his hand. He was already planning to call his partner when his phone lit up with a call from her. He brought it to his ear, closing the other one with the tip of his finger to ward off the sound of the buzzsaws. "Hey, you. Everything—"

He paused. He was going to ask her if everything was okay. But that sounded too close to asking if she was okay, and she'd already gotten pissed at him for asking that one too many times.

He started to add, "Turn out all right?" when she spoke over him. The reception wasn't great, so he could barely make out her words. "Hold on." He got into his car and rolled up the windows, deadening the sound of the saws. "Say that again, would you?"

"I said that I just finished talking to Laura Porter's primary care physician. He says that she just went on the medication recently and while it's serious if she doesn't have it, it's not our biggest concern."

He stared up at the ceiling of the car, understanding trickling in. The other two murdered girls, Joy and Nevaeh, were only missing a couple days before their bodies were found. While some killers loved to hang onto their victims, toying with them, this killer wouldn't wait that long. "Our biggest concern is the guy who's got her."

"Exactly." She let out a breath, and he could tell she was getting antsy. "Did you have any luck?"

"Yeah, actually. Not sure what it'll turn up, but I have the name of a guy who lives out in the woods. A logger said he has been pretty weird and all but withdrawn from society recently. I think it's worth checking out. Want me to come get you before I go, or were you planning to interview Dr. Benson?"

"No. Most of the doctors are out. I don't want to wait here any longer than I have to," she said. "Pick me up."

"Will do," he said, ending the call. That was exactly what he wanted to do, anyway. He'd feel much better with his other half on the case with him.

CHAPTER SIXTEEN

"Bo Rupert," Nora announced, reading the file from her cell phone. "Yep. You're right. He has a police record a mile long. But he disappeared off the grid two years ago."

"What's he been booked for?"

"Everything from petty theft to assault of a minor. Apparently, as much of a loner as he is, he's big into harassing young women who want nothing to do with him."

"Interesting," Snyder said, pressing on the gas as they wound through the dirt roads. "Sounds promising. This is definitely off the grid. I hope you know how to get back, because I almost didn't make it out of here the first time to pick you up."

"Of course. I'm great with directions."

Nora was navigating, but even though it was midday, and they were using the car's headlights, it felt like nighttime. She suppressed a shudder as they turned onto a narrower road, and it grew darker still. As they continued on, the road bent, and the first signs of a roof, covered in old, worn brick-red tiles and dried leaves, came into view. Smoke from a chimney pipe wafted into the air.

"This looks like our place," Snyder said, laying off the gas. "And it looks like someone is home."

"Stop here," she instructed him. "If he's the guy we're looking for, and he's got Laura Porter, I get the feeling he's not going to be too friendly."

"Good call," he said, braking. Taking a deep breath, he reached for the door handle, and she did the same.

It was impossible not to make noise. Though it was mid-summer, the ground was covered with dried leaves. Nora learned as much the second she stepped out, and the debris under her foot made a loud crunching nose. By the time they joined each other at the front of the car, the element of surprise had significantly diminished.

Still, the house stood quiet. The porch was empty, except for some strewn muddy boots and an old rifle. There was no sign of life, save for the smoke billowing from the small chimney pipe on the roof.

"What do you think?" she asked him in a low voice.

"Let's just do this thing. We're just here to talk, right? No problem."

She nodded. It sounded like a good plan. And yet, as she stood there, looking at the old, dark-wood cabin, that creeping sense of déjà vu once again began to invade.

She hardly realized he'd advanced on the cabin until he turned back. He said nothing, but she could sense the words, "You okay?" on his lips.

Quickly, she caught up.

The closer they got to the front porch, the more dilapidated the old shack appeared. The planks of wood were rotting away, and the slats in the front porch were strung with so many spider webs, packed with dead insects and leaves, that it was impossible to see through any of them. One of the front windows must've been broken and replaced with a plywood panel. Dried leaves were packed like snowdrifts into every corner, and there was a sour, sickly sweet, and somewhat metallic scent in the air.

It smelled like rotting flesh.

Déjà vu, all over again.

It hit her like a thunderclap headache when she raised a foot to take the first step onto the porch. Instead, she covered her nose with her hand and reeled back, staggering slightly before grabbing hold of the railing. Pieces of it splintered and fell apart in her hand, but it still gave her the support she desperately needed.

Snyder looked back, and she whispered, hoarse, "Do you smell that?"

He nodded, his face grave, and took a step. She'd never been able to let him best her, so she followed and overtook him, reaching the top of the stairs first.

We're just going to have a conversation. No problem, she reminded herself, looking for a doorbell. When she didn't find one, she rapped on the center of the door.

Then she listened. She heard the shifting of floorboards inside, but no one answered.

She knocked again, louder.

When there was no answer, this time, she stepped closer and pressed her ear near the crack in the door. At first, she heard nothing, but then she heard a sound, a soft but high-pitched tone. It sounded like a tea kettle just before it was about to boil.

Her eyes found Jason's. "What is it?" he asked.

She inhaled, unsure, and caught a more pungent whiff of that terrible, wrong scent. Instinctively, she reached for her gun, just as the high-pitched sound became an unmistakably female moan. It sounded like a woman in distress.

Heart racing, Nora pressed her ear closer and wrapped her fingers around the butt of her sidearm. At that moment, she heard the voice beg, unmistakably, "No, please! Oh, please, please!"

Laura.

"She's in there!" Nora shouted, reaching frantically for the doorknob. She grabbed at it and turned it, but it wouldn't budge. Shoving at it, she cried to her partner, "We have to get in there."

Taking that cue, Jason nudged her aside and backed up, battering the door with his shoulder. Once, twice. The door shuddered in its frame, more each time, before finally exploding open. Jason staggered inside with it and let out an anguished yell. "Oh, hell."

Nora stumbled over him to see, but realized it was more about the smell. Or stench, rather. It was overpowering. Blinking the tears in her eyes and pinching her nose, she caught sight of exactly what was causing the rancid odor.

Skinned animal hides were draped over every surface—chair backs, kitchen counters, sofas, an old box television set, railings, a portable clothes-drying rack made of wooden dowels. The room was dark, and the stench was almost a visible cloud of haze in the darkness, invading her nostrils even with them pinched closed. Nora grabbed the front of her blazer and brought the fabric over her face as she peered into the murk.

Nobody. The room was empty. And yet, she was sure she'd heard …

Just then, a female voice rose up, whimpering. Now, closer, Nora realized it sounded different. And she could pinpoint exactly where it was coming from—on the other side of a single wood-paneled door across from the kitchen.

She motioned to Jason, who effortlessly fell in line, backing her up, as she lifted her gun and skirted around the animal-skin-draped furniture. Their eyes silently communicated the plan as she pressed against the door frame, gun at the ready.

Taking a deep breath, she counted down in her head: *One, two …*

On three, she grabbed the doorknob and twisted, then charged inside in one swift movement, raising her gun and shouting, "FBI. Freeze! Hands up!"

The room was dark, except for one thing—a television set in the corner. Her eyes fell on the two naked bodies on the screen, and her mind cycled in confusion as she turned to the only person in the room—a chubby, elderly man in a dirty wife-beater and boxer shorts, who jumped off of his bed and did exactly as she said, eyes wide. "Don't shoot! Please."

She stared in the darkness at the frightened man, who'd wedged himself in a corner of the room, trembling. "Bo Rupert?" she asked.

He nodded. "What I done?" he asked, baring a set of crooked, rotten teeth. Other than that, he looked nothing like what she'd expected. She'd been hoping for some similarities to the sketch Miranda had provided, but this man, though slovenly and fat and hairy and distasteful, didn't match at all.

Jason lowered his gun and looked around the room. "It's just you here?"

The man slowly nodded. "I live alone. Just enjoying some adult entertainment. Is my right, yeah?"

Nora's excitement over the possible lead had already waned. Her annoyance only grew as the woman on the television continued making noises. They clearly weren't those of someone who was in peril. Which meant that this guy was just a creep, and had nothing to do with the case.

"Yeah, dude," Jason said, going to the old set and flipping off the television.

"Hey, I was watching that," the man said, with only a little fight in him.

"Not right now. Right now, I want to talk to you," Nora said, looking around the room. The bed was covered in dingy sheets, and there were piles of clothes and dirty dishes around the room. There was also a strong scent of urine, even stronger than the stench of rotten meat outside.

"What about?" he asked, scratching at his substantial stomach.

Flies skittered around, past Nora's line of vision. She waved them away and lowered the gun, hoping to salvage something good from this interaction. "You've been living out here alone a long time?"

He nodded.

"Notice anything different? Have you seen any people driving past, any unusual activity?"

He picked up his sagging old boxers and pulled them tight around his flabby waist. "Lady, I don't see nothing. And I like it that way.

You're the first real people I see in months. I like the TV 'cause it don't talk back to me."

He let out a phlegmy *har har har* of a laugh, which disintegrated into a wet cough, and didn't bother to cover his mouth. Instead, he reached for the bottom of his wife-beater and used it to wipe his mouth, baring rolls upon rolls of hairy flab.

Jason eyed him in disgust. "You do some hunting, though."

"Sure do," he said, standing straighter with pride. "You seen my hides, huh? I sell them. That's how I'm able to make my money and keep in this paradise of a house."

"Okay, so you must see someone for that," Nora pointed out.

He shook his head. "Ain't sold anything in months. And my contacts come here. I got one coming in August to take my inventory off my hands and give me a big, fat check."

It was hard to believe anyone could want that stinking, rancid mess outside. Jason said, "You ever think about keeping that stuff outside?"

"Nah. Too humid out there. And I don't want no one stealing stuff from me."

"Have you seen anyone like that? People you thought were poachers, or trespassers, recently?"

He shook his head. "But you never know."

"And you have been out hunting," Nora pointed out. "You must know these woods pretty well. Have you seen anything out of the ordinary?"

His brow wrinkled in concentration. "Saw a deer with two heads once. But I'd been drinking. My shot went wide, and he ran off."

Jason cleared his throat. "Yeah, but any people? Trespassers? Maybe a man came by to check out your cabin?"

Nora looked at Bo, eager for his answer. It was a good question; she wished she'd thought of it. If the suspect was taking people out to random backwoods cabins to commit his crimes, there was a good chance that maybe he'd scouted this one out.

But Bo shook his head. "Nope. Never saw no one like that."

The two agents sighed in unison. Jason gave Bo a card to call, in case the man saw anything during his hunting trips, but Nora knew it was in vain. After all, all the way out in these woods, Bo likely didn't even have a phone. But he'd nodded with excitement, likely happy that he was no longer under their suspicion, as he walked them to the door. "Of course, Agents, anything I can do to help!"

When they got to the car, Nora looked at her partner. "It was a good idea."

He started the engine and did a K-turn to head back the way they'd come. "Not good enough, apparently. Where next?"

She shrugged. There were a number of avenues they could pursue, but none of them felt very hot. They could interview the victims' friends, acquaintances, people who had been nearby when the kidnappings occurred. But the police had done all of that, and already uncovered very little.

"I hate to say it," Jason said, when they finally emerged from the labyrinth of woods about a half-hour later, "but your idea of going to that group session might be the best one we have."

Nora sighed and checked her phone. The session was at five, and it wasn't even mid-afternoon. She wasn't okay with just waiting for it, especially with Laura Porter missing and the moments ticking away. But she could be anywhere, in the vast expanse of woods in Blackburn County. They had to make progress … somehow.

"Let's stop somewhere to get something to eat, get out the map and start putting the locations on it, see if we can make some connections," she suggested, but it sounded like a shot in the dark.

Somewhere out there, a woman was fighting for her life. And the last thing Nora needed was to feel responsible for another failure, not when she had the power to stop this killer, once and for all.

CHAPTER SEVENTEEN

Laura Porter woke to find herself in something most people would've thought was their worst nightmare. But because she had lived through one before, she knew better.

Sometimes, even years after the incident, she dreamt about it. Lying helpless on the hard floor, as the world around her went up in flames.

Now, though, she wasn't lying on the hardwood floor of her living room, watching the drapes and the walls igniting. Now, her cheek was pressed against a chalky, dirt floor. The gray dust billowed around her face every time she breathed out, and it clung to her nostrils. The walls around her were dingy gray cinderblocks. A single, dim bulb swayed overhead, and she could make out cobweb-covered rafters in the shadows.

As she sprawled on her stomach, her head aching from the blow, her skin tight and crusted over with dried blood, she said a silent prayer of thanks for one thing: that her family wasn't there to experience this with her.

Because this was a terror she'd rather not share.

Her mind cycled back to her last memory, back at home—making that tomato sandwich, then going to the door to make sure it had been locked. Her gut somersaulted as she remembered the footprints, that sudden bolt of fear that had struck her when she realized she wasn't alone. The hands, wrapping around her, the scream that had caught in her throat. And then …

Then she'd woken up here. She didn't know where "here" was, but she knew that it meant something very bad had happened.

Scattered thoughts swarmed her mind. *Who did this? Will anyone be looking for me? Am I all alone here?* But the one that rooted in her head was the most important… *How do I get out?*

She wanted to investigate her surroundings more, but her body wasn't cooperating. Her arms and legs were useless; she couldn't even be sure if they were still attached. The mere act of rolling over felt like an impossible feat. Instead, since one eye was pressed into the ground, she let her other eye wander around, trying to take in as much of the room as possible.

Small. Dark. No furnishings except a single wooden table in the center of the room. From her vantage point, she couldn't see what was on it. There was also a wooden ladder, attached to what had to be a hatch in the ceiling.

Basement. I'm in someone's basement.

And soon after that:

That's the way I'm going to get out of here.

With that thought in mind, she bit down hard on her lip and tried to summon the energy to move. Instead, all that happened was that she let out a long, tortured moan of exertion.

That was when she heard the sound of someone, or something, moving behind her.

A lock of her hair blocked the way, so she couldn't see the back half of the room. She'd assumed she was alone here.

Clearly, she'd assumed wrong.

Because at that moment, she heard definite footfalls and the sound of someone's heavy breathing.

She remembered how she'd begged just two years ago. *Please,* she'd pleaded, her voice as dry as sandpaper. *Please don't hurt me. There has to be some mistake. I don't have anything you could want. Have mercy on me.*

Back then, she'd started to sob, hoping that would make a difference, that they would take pity on her.

But not now. Now, she knew that sometimes people were evil down to the core, and there was nothing she could do to change it. Nothing she could say. Now, she wanted to face this evil man. She wanted to know her captor. That was the one thing she'd always wished she'd had the courage to do during the home invasion—she'd wanted to face those thugs, unblinking, and spit in their faces. Because if anyone deserved such treatment, it was them.

But when the face of her new captor appeared in front of her, the fight went clear out of her.

The face in front of her was not human. It was a ghoul.

She blinked, sure it was just a trick of the light, but the features only became ghastlier. Red pinpoint eyes, pale skin, like something out of a monster movie. She let out a cry of horror and snapped her eyes shut as a robotic voice hummed out, "Pretty thing. Worthless thing. Are you scared yet?"

Laura didn't speak. She squeezed her eyes tighter, willing herself to be brave.

“You should be,” it hissed out. “Because when I come back, I’m going to kill you.”

CHAPTER EIGHTEEN

Nora took a single bite of her greasy, overcooked hamburger and tossed it down on the plate, disgusted. "Just great."

They were sitting in the back of the Blackburn Diner, a greasy spoon they went to far too often whenever they needed to think on a case. There, the coffee was strong, and there was never a crowd, so even at the height of the lunch hour, they could usually get a booth far from the rest of the clientele.

Now, she stared at the map, where they'd marked all the pertinent locations—where the two bodies were found, the victims' homes, the cabin Miranda had escaped from. The woods in the center of Blackburn made a big, empty green spot on the map, and Miranda's cabin was there. The other locations were on the outskirts of the county. But the map didn't give any clue as to their next steps.

"So what are we looking at here?" Jason said, twisting the map to get a better view.

"I'll tell you what. A whole lot of nothing," she moaned, gulping lukewarm coffee to wash down the taste of the burger and try to wake up some of her brain cells.

He dragged a hand down his face. "That's what I thought. But there's got to be something we're missing."

She shook her head. "I think there's *a lot* of something, probably."

"The thugs who killed Porter's family were members of a gang, right?" Jason noted. When she nodded, he said, "Maybe we should look into them. This might be a vendetta for her putting them behind bars."

Nora let out a long breath. "So you think Laura's kidnapping might have nothing to do with the other murders?"

He nodded.

She hated to agree with him, but the connections they'd made between all four incidents were tenuous at best. Maybe they were grasping at straws.

The waitress, Becky, who usually left them alone but knew them well enough to understand when they needed something, stopped by. "Can I get you anything else, honey?"

Nora nodded. "Pie, please."

"Black bottom banana cream?"

"Yes. With whipped cream."

"Make that two," Jason said, leaning forward and giving her a concerned look. Whenever she wanted pie, it had to be pretty bad.

"You got it," Becky said, taking Jason's empty plate and heading off.

Nora sighed and sat back, her muscles tense with frustration. "I *hate* this."

"What part of *this* are you talking about?"

"Oh, that delightful part where we're just sitting around with our thumbs up our butts while a woman is somewhere nearby, probably being tortured to death," she said in a low voice. "It sucks."

He opened his mouth, likely to give her one of his famous Snyder Pep Talks, which usually did make her feel better, but her phone started to ring in her pocket. The display showed a strange number from their area code. She held up a finger before he could get a word out and pressed the phone to her ear. "Yes?"

The voice was female, familiar, but Nora couldn't quite place it. "Is this Detective Nora Price?"

"Yes, this is Special Agent Price. Who's this?"

"This is Elle Squires. Remember? The therapist who does the breakthrough group therapies in her home?"

Nora glanced at Jason, who was following the conversation closely. Of course, the meeting was tonight, and the therapist was probably wondering if she'd decided on coming. There was only so much space in her living room, after all. "Oh, right, we were just talking about you. I—"

"How are you?" she said, in a very practiced, concerned voice, just like the therapist she was.

"Good, good. Actually, my partner and I were planning on coming tonight, if that's not too much—"

"Oh, not at all, that's actually really great. I'd wanted to talk to you, anyway. I was just checking out the news, hoping to see more about the case, and I realized something that could help you. Can you come earlier, say at four?"

Nora checked the time. She was almost out of ideas, so she didn't want to wait that long. "Sure … what is this about?"

"I saw the television report on Laura Porter. They showed her photograph on the news. And it just clicked. I'm pretty sure I saw her. She came to one of my group meetings a month ago, to deal with her grief over losing her family, but she never signed up for the actual therapy itself. So it got me thinking …"

Nora sat up straight. "Thinking about what?"

"Well, my therapies are very popular, sometimes standing room only, and I don't charge people who just want to come in and see what it's about. I don't even take names or numbers. They can show up anonymously. And so I thought, maybe Nevaeh Hudson did come to one of them, after all. I just wouldn't know."

The waitress came with their pies, but Nora no longer wanted to drown her frustrations in it. This was it. A lead. The first real, promising one they'd had. "You said that sometimes people are cured in one session. Do you happen to have any frequent attendees?"

"Agent Price, yes, my therapies are very well-received. But I do have many people who are, how shall we say, reluctant to go under my care. And so they come to observe. I don't limit the number of times they can observe. I want them to be comfortable. So yes, many people have been there multiple times."

"Do you record the sessions you have, by any chance?"

"Of course."

Nora pumped her fist a little in excitement.

"Hold on," she said into the phone, motioning to Becky to bring her the check. "We'll be over in a little bit."

She ended the call and started piling the papers into her backpack.

"You going to tell me what that's all about?" Jason asked as he reached into his wallet to pay for their lunch.

"She told me that the sessions she conducts are open, and pretty crowded. She thinks she *might* just have seen Laura Porter there, a month or so ago," Nora said, throwing the bag over her shoulder and heading for the exit. Not checking to see if he was behind her, she added, "And though she doesn't remember her, she thinks it's possible Nevaeh Hudson might have been there, too."

When she reached the car, she realized Jason wasn't there. He ran to catch up with her. "Wait. Why didn't she tell us this before?"

Nora shrugged. "Who knows? Maybe she truthfully didn't think of it. But anyway, if this connection is real, it means someone at the sessions might have met these women. He knows they're wounded, thinks of them as easy targets. And he goes after them."

"So we're going over there?" he said, climbing into the car.

"Yeah, we'll review the sessions on video, see what we can find. And with any luck, maybe he'll show up at tonight's session, too. And we can grab him."

*

Nora stared at the darkened screen. A number of people, in silhouette, had spoken about their traumas, and now a man was discussing his harrowing fear of snakes.

Jason said, "So all the videos are this way?"

Elle Squires nodded.

They were huddled around a small computer screen, and Nora sighed, feeling all of her triumph draining away. "When you said you had video of the session, I thought you'd captured it so that we could identify the people in the room."

"Oh, no," she said, her eyes wide. "I wouldn't do that, for confidentiality's sake. Most of these people don't want their struggles to get out. They're ashamed of them. I use these videos for promotional purposes."

Nora looked at Jason, feeling defeated. She shoved away from the desk, stood up, and began to pace. "But you're sure you saw Laura Porter at one of your sessions?"

To Nora's ultimate chagrin, Elle Squires began to backtrack. "Well, like I said, I conduct so many of these. I said I thought she *might* have been at one of these sessions."

"Do you have audio of her talking about her experience?" Nora suggested.

"Oh, no. It's only the people who sign up for the therapy that get that. If she did come, she was just an observer."

Nora rolled her eyes to the ceiling and let out a groan.

Jason's phone buzzed, and he looked at it, then typed something in. He motioned to Nora and took her aside. "Hey. I decided to check into that gang that was associated with the Porter family murder. Turns out there is an ex–gang member who's willing to talk to me. I think I should meet with him."

"Sounds a little dangerous," she said. "I should come—"

"Stay here," he told her, more of a command than a request. "The guy might still show up to the meeting."

She nodded and said goodbye to him. Then she looked at Elle Squires. "Is there anyone who attends your meetings who has given you a bad vibe?"

Elle thought for a moment, then nodded. "There's a man who comes almost every week. He's tall, bald, kind of serious-looking. At first, I thought he was interested in the therapies, but he never asks me about them. He just sits there, in the back corner, and watches. I suppose some might think he's creepy."

Nora looked at the clock. It was 4:30 p.m., almost time for the session to begin. She only hoped that she would be able to stop thinking about her own past long enough to help find Laura Porter.

CHAPTER NINETEEN

Nora sat in the corner of the dimly lit room, sinking into a beanbag chair, as the participants began to arrive. Ordinarily, she tried to hide her trauma and present herself as a typical FBI agent, but here, every time someone looked at her, she had the feeling they were seeing right through her—not noticing her trauma, but that she was FBI.

She sipped some sugary juice from a small paper cup as other people filled the room, stopping at the refreshment table before finding a spot among the cushions. By the time five o'clock rolled around, it was just as Elle had said—the place was standing room only. People shared cushions and packed close to one another, and yet, the doorway was clogged with observers.

"Come on in, make room, make room," Elle instructed from her spot at the front of the room. "Welcome! Welcome!"

Nervous chatter rose up as the people eventually settled into their spaces. The room, once comfortable, began to get oppressively warm. Nora tugged at her collar as she pulled her legs up to give another person more room. *Sure hope no one here suffers from claustrophobia.*

Elle Squires clapped her hands and the room immediately silenced. She looked around the room, her eyes full of sympathy. "Now, I'm so glad you all could join me. If everyone is ready, I'd like to begin."

Immediately, she had the attention of every person in the room. No one moved; it was almost as if they were all holding their breaths, waiting to hear more.

"Thank you to those who have come out to observe. Today we have six individuals who are in the process of reinventing themselves." She motioned to the six individuals sitting in the front row and smiled warmly at each of them. "I say *reinventing*, rather than recovering from trauma … because that is what we ultimately want to do. Trauma leaves scars, and to pretend we can erase them is a lie. But you can come out of it stronger than before. Please, Meredith, tell us why you're here."

A woman with long, graying hair spoke in a gravelly voice. "I've had three husbands and countless relationships. Each one of the men I chose to be with was abusive to me. I've been told time and time again that I'm not responsible for the way men act toward me, but with every failed relationship, I became more and more desperate, more and more certain I was unlovable. Now, I rarely leave the house. I want to reinvent myself, to believe in myself again."

Elle leaned forward and put a hand on the woman's shoulder. "Thank you for sharing. Next, we have Tyson. Tyson, please share your story."

One by one, the individuals at the front of the room shared their personal stories of woe. Each one was sadder than the next. Nora tried to concentrate on the case, on scoping out the room for possible suspects. But her mind always swept back to Elle Squires, who, quietly confident, sat at the head of the room, giving her patients gentle encouragement. So far, nothing had seemed very groundbreaking. *Does this lady really think she can help these people with one session?*

Nora shifted and scolded herself. *That's not what you're here for. You're here to find a killer.*

She tried to tune out the program at the front of the room and instead scanned the faces of the various attendees. Sure enough, she noticed a man standing in the very corner of the room, watching intently.

For the first time, Nora narrowed in on him, and not the program. He was tall, his face pale and square, his eyes dark and beady, somewhat like the sketch Miranda had provided. There was something unsettling about the way he watched, his breathing rapid, a small smile on his face, almost as if he was getting a thrill from watching these people relate their worst tragedies. Not only was he watching the proceedings, but he was also watching the people, just like Nora was. He seemed to be scanning the faces for someone in particular. At one point, she noticed that he set his sights on a young woman seated on a cushion near the refreshment stand. Pretty and pert-nosed, her long red hair tied up in a ponytail, the girl sat with her chin on her knees, unaware of the man's leering.

Nora's pulse thrummed beneath her skin. *That's him. That's got to be him. I'm sure of it.*

No sooner had that thought occurred to her than his eyes shifted, landing straight on her. Their gazes locked, and Nora felt the heat climbing its way up her neck.

She looked away, at the therapist delivering her program. Apparently, she'd missed a lot. Now, Elle stood in front of one of the participants, her hands on either side of her head, whispering into her ear. From here, Nora could see the woman's eyes were closed, fluttering like a hummingbird's wings. All of the participants, in fact, had their eyes closed. The observers watched, rapt, hardly daring to breathe.

Nora looked back at the redhead, who hadn't moved, so interested was she in the program. Then she allowed her eyes to flit toward the man.

But he was gone.

Frantic, Nora scanned the room, but he was nowhere to be found. She looked toward the door and saw movement there.

"Damn," she said under her breath, causing a number of people to glare at her as she struggled from the cross-legged position to her knees and crawled toward the exit. She stepped on more than a couple body parts on the way, and a man muttered, "Hey, watch it."

"Sorry, just need to get out," she explained, moving faster, wincing over the commotion she was causing. But she simply couldn't let this guy get away.

Finally, when mercifully, she reached the door, she brought herself upright and tried to squeeze through. Though most people in the foyer were still watching the program and shifted their heads in annoyance around her to see, one man, who was pushed up against a corner near the door, smiled at her.

"Not your cup of tea?" he whispered.

"No." She looked at him as he sidestepped away from the door to let her out of it. He was a clean-cut, handsome man with a goatee and a button-down shirt, who looked like he'd just come from the office. "But thanks."

She opened the door and looked out toward the elevator. The man was already gone. He must've taken the stairs. *Damn.*

Or had he left at all? She looked back toward the closed door of the restroom. Maybe he'd gone there.

The clean-cut man was still watching her, so she whispered, "Did you happen to see a guy go out here?"

He nodded. "Guess it wasn't his cup of tea, either." He shrugged. "Though Elle says he's here all the time."

Nora gritted her teeth. That had to have been the guy, then. She'd missed her chance.

Hadn't she?

But before she could take off toward the stairs, the man held a hand out to her. "I'm Dane."

She shook it absently. "Nora." She took a step toward the stairwell. She didn't want to be impolite, but she had to go. As she was about to leave, though, something he said stood out to her. He was the first strange man who'd ever talked to her who didn't give off vibes that made her want to run in the other direction. In fact, a part of her *really* wanted to stay and chat. "You've been here before?"

He shook his head. "First time. I met Elle at a coffee shop and she suggested I come by. She's really good at getting people to open up. Had me nearly crying into my coffee at the café." He laughed. "Figured I needed to see what this was all about."

She smiled, and something in his eyes, or his pleasant face, captivated her so much, she almost forgot about the creep she'd wanted to tail. She realized that she still had her hand in his, and pulled it away. "I've got to go."

"Too bad. See you, Nora," he called after her in a light, pleasant tone, as she raced down the hallway in search of her suspect.

Throwing open the door, she ran into the stairwell and leaned over, looking as far as she could down the stairs. Nothing.

The stairwell was entirely clear; she didn't even hear the sound of footfalls on the steps. By the time she reached the bottom floor and exploded out into the lobby of the apartment building, she was sure this was all in vain.

Stupid, Nora. Real stupid. You got so captivated by a pair of warm brown eyes that you forgot yourself. What are you, in middle school?

As she headed for the revolving door, her shoes smacking against the polished tile floor of the lobby, she thought of the many parking garages the creepy man could be headed off to, scattered around the building. He was probably in his car by now, minutes away from returning to Laura and ending her life.

And Nora could've prevented it.

A sick feeling swirled in her gut as she retreated out into the warm, humid night. Rain had fallen, and now, pockets of mist hung over the wet, empty streets, clinging to the streetlights, lending an eerie, foreboding ambience to the area.

She looked around, trying to decide which direction to take, when she spotted a hunched figure pressed up against the wall, his back to her. The orange light of a match illuminated his features just enough for her to make them out as he lit a cigarette.

It was him.

As she moved closer, he flicked the newly lit cigarette into the gutter and took off in the other direction.

She followed. "Excuse me."

He didn't turn around. In fact, he moved faster.

“Excuse me,” she said, louder.

He had to have heard that one. And yet, he started to walk even faster.

As she tracked him, picking up the pace until she was nearly at a run, she noted as he passed under the streetlights that he was wearing jeans and a coat, despite the warm night. He had his collar pulled up around his neck, as if he was up to no good. And he was running from her. If that wasn’t a dead giveaway that something was suspicious, she didn’t know what was.

“I just want to talk to you!” she shouted at him.

He looked over his shoulder, then broke into a run.

Nearly out of breath, she grabbed her gun from her shoulder holster and took aim. “FBI! Freeze!”

Instantly, he stopped and raised his hands skyward.

“Turn around,” she ordered.

He did as she instructed. “I didn’t do anything wrong.”

“Where are you headed in such a rush, then?”

He hitched a shoulder. “Nowhere. Just don’t want to talk to no one. And you looked like a cop. I can tell one when I see one. Saw you in that meeting, watching me. And I didn’t like it.”

“Why were you in that meeting?” she asked, moving closer. “Apparently, you’ve been going to a lot of them.”

“That a crime?” he challenged. “I was invited.”

“You have some unresolved trauma?”

“Don’t we all?” he said, letting out a laugh that echoed through the quiet streets. “Nah. But that girl, Elle? I like her.”

“I saw you looking at a couple of the girls,” she noted, taking another step closer, her gun still aimed. “Why’s that?”

“Far as I know, that’s no crime,” he said with an insolent shrug. “You expecting to arrest me for something, Agent? Or are you just out to harass law-abiding citizens?”

As she moved forward, she noticed something bulging on his ankle. The hem of his jeans was caught in it.

It was an ankle monitor.

All the breath seemed to leave Nora’s lungs as she studied it. “What’s that for?”

He shrugged. “Bunch of things. Assault, theft … but I haven’t done anything wrong. You can tell my probation officer that I’ve been the picture of a good citizen.”

She sighed. She wouldn’t go that far, but the fact was, this wasn’t her man. Couldn’t be her man. *And anyway, why would you think the killer would be out scouting for his next victim? At this moment, he's probably getting ready to kill Laura Porter. And you're wasting time.*

Dropping her weapon, she turned and headed back up the street, grabbing her phone to call her partner. She only hoped Jason's investigation had been more worthwhile, because the clock was still ticking, and with the way the other cases had gone, she had a good feeling that tonight might be Laura Porter's last.

CHAPTER TWENTY

Nora frowned as she leaned back in the passenger's seat of Jason's car. Misery loved company, but for Laura's sake, she'd hoped her partner would have had better luck. "And that was it?"

They were idling outside the apartment building, watching people spilling out the doors. The therapy session must've just ended. She pulled her blazer over her front, hoping one of them would look like a demented serial killer who targeted young women. But in the darkness, they all looked the same.

And now they were scattering all over the town, going who-knows-where.

"Yep. A total dead end, waste of time. The former gang member didn't know anything about the Porter case. He was just looking for a way to cut a deal for a drug charge he's facing. As far as I can tell, all of the gang members involved were put away." He tilted his head back against the headrest and blew out a long breath of air. "So yours was no better?"

"It's better in the sense that I still think that the murders must have something to do with those sessions. I know we don't know for sure that all of the victims attended them, but it's the best shot we have. The only problem is," she muttered, slamming her closed fist onto her thigh, "I guess I went after the wrong creep. *Dammit!*"

He shook his head. "Don't beat yourself up. We'll go to another session. Together."

"And by then, Laura will be dead," Nora said, facing the window so her partner couldn't see the tears in her eyes. In the race against time, they were too far away from the finish line to even think about winning.

"You didn't see any other potential suspects?" he asked.

She let out a groan of annoyance. "We were packed in like sardines. I could barely see anything. I made the mistake of focusing in on that guy and pretty much ignored everyone else. And now, they're all gone. But no one else really stood out to me. They were all—normal, I guess?"

He rolled his eyes. "I hate normal people."

"Yeah, well, I guess they're not, if they're there to deal with past trauma. But they're good at hiding that they're not. The only thing is, there had to have been at least fifty people in that room and we don't have a way of getting in touch with a single one of them." This time, she slammed *both* closed fists into her thighs. "Talk about a complete missed opportunity. But you know what?"

"What?" His eyes found hers in the dark cabin of the sedan.

"What if he wasn't there at all? It only occurred to me afterwards that if he'd already kidnapped a victim, he wouldn't be scouting out a new one just yet. Not unless …"

"Unless she was already dead," Jason muttered, and let out a heavy breath.

"Yep." She sighed, trying to force that thought out of her mind. She really didn't want to think about that. She checked her phone. "I hate to say it, but you know what I think we should do?"

"Go to the liquor store and share a bottle of Jack?" He smirked.

"Would love to," she said, shaking her head. The sidewalk outside the apartment building was now deserted; the last stragglers had disappeared. "But I think we should go in and talk to Elle. See if she noticed anything odd."

Jason reached for the door handle. "Let's do this thing, then."

They hurried across the street and into the lobby of the building, then took the elevator up to the woman's apartment. As they walked down the hallway, Nora noticed Elle Squires's door was open, and she was talking to a patient in the doorway.

As she drew closer, Nora recognized her as the older woman with the history of abusive relationships, the first patient to be introduced. Her cheeks were streaked with tears and she was holding Elle's hands tightly. "Again, I can't thank you enough."

Elle stroked her arm. "It's my pleasure, dear. Have a safe trip home."

Smiling wide, the woman headed toward the elevator, ignoring the agents. Jason raised an eyebrow. "One satisfied customer, I see."

Elle waved at them. "Hi, Agents." She looked at Nora. "So, have you decided to participate in my next session?"

Nora shook her head. Truthfully, the temptation was pulling at her, but she had other things on her mind right now. "Not quite yet. But I have to admit, it was impressive. Well, what I saw."

Elle beamed. "Yes, well, like I said, it's very fulfilling to help people the way I do. Care to come in?"

The agents went into the living area. The room was now clear, but it was still stuffy, and there were empty cups of juice and plates scattered about. Elle started to stack them, moving gracefully about the room in her flowing dress. "Sit. There are still some cookies left, if you'd like. Juice. Is there something else I can help you two with?"

"Yes, I was just wondering if you noticed anything or anyone odd at tonight's session? Anything at all that stood out?" Nora asked, glancing around the room before deciding she'd stand rather than attempt to sit on one of those floor cushions.

She frowned. "No. But I don't know if you noticed that creepy guy …? In the corner? He was there."

Nora nodded. "Yes. I looked into him. He checked out."

"Oh. Really?" She shrugged. "Other than that, I can't imagine … sorry if I led you on a wild goose chase, there."

"No, it's all right," Jason said, grabbing a cookie from the table. "So there was no one unusual tonight at all? No one mentioned anything to you that seemed off?"

Elle finished stacking the plates and shook her head. "Not that I can recall. It was a pretty standard night. A little busier than usual, but that's about it. Sorry."

Jason looked at Nora, who merely scraped her teeth over her upper lip. She was out of ideas.

He then rushed forward to help Elle, who was attempting to wrangle the dirty plates into a plastic trash bag.

"Sorry if I seem a little harried," she said as she tied the top of the bag. "I have to type all this up and get it to a colleague. He's analyzing the results for a paper he's doing, and I believe it's due to his editor tomorrow morning."

"A colleague?" Nora asked. "I thought you worked on this alone."

"Well, I'm not a medical professional," Elle explained. "Dr. Fitzsimmons, at the university, provides that side of things. He and I are writing a research paper for the *Journal of Modern Psychiatry*, and it's always best to have the most up-to-date data."

Dr. Fitzsimmons. Of the myriad psychiatrists Nora had gone through over the years, that one stood out. The man looked the part of a psychiatric doctor—tall and imposing, with bushy salt-and-pepper hair, glasses. He always wore a tweed blazer and smelled like pipe smoke, and had a habit of grumbling under his breath too often.

Nora knew him well. He'd been the third—or was it the fourth?—psychiatrist she'd kicked to the curb.

"You mean Dr. Mark Fitzsimmons? Of Carlton University?"

Nora asked the question even though she already knew the answer. There was only one university in the county, and the esteemed Dr. Fitzsimmons had been the chair of his department. She'd been intimidated by his stuffy office, full of diplomas and papers he'd penned and photographs of himself with important people. It had only taken her one meeting to decide this guy was not for her.

So when Elle nodded, she wasn't surprised.

She looked at Jason, that fire inside her igniting again. When his gaze met hers, he mouthed, *What?*

I'll tell you later, she mouthed back.

"Well, we won't keep you any longer, then," Nora said, quickly making her way to the door.

When they had said their goodbyes to the therapist and were out in the hallway, Nora practically burst, speaking a mile a minute to get her partner up to speed. "Dr. Fitzsimmons is like a fixture in this area's psychiatric community."

Jason raised an eyebrow. "Good for him? What are you, a fangirl?"

She nudged him with her elbow. "*No,*" she said pointedly, though she had to admit, her voice was rising to that of an overly excited, screechy teenager. "Quite the opposite. But I have met him. And while he might not look like the sketch Miranda provided, we've got to think. That creep from the ice cream shop might not be the killer. It could be someone else. And Dr. Fitzsimmons has worked with tons of therapists, all over the area. He trained them. Which means—"

"He knows their patients' cases," Jason finished with a nod. "So, you were a patient of his?"

"Can't say that," she said, jabbing the elevator button with excitement. "I only went to one session with him."

"You didn't click?"

"Far from it. He had this creepy way of gurgling in the back of his throat before he said anything, and there was something just—I don't know. *Off* about him."

They stepped into the elevator, and he shrugged. "Well. Guess it's as good a lead as any."

Her spirits deflated as he pulled out his phone and started to type something in. He was probably right. All of the other leads had gotten her excited and led absolutely nowhere. This man was a respected psychiatrist, probably the most respected in the whole county. It was too much to think he could also be a serial killer, as well.

But as they stepped out into the lobby, Jason, nose still buried in his phone, said, "Hmm."

She looked over at him, only half-interested. It had been a long night already.

"He's lived his whole life in the county. Specializes in abnormal psychology and violent crimes. And not only is he connected to Squires, he also provided a quote for the *Daily Bullet* about the killer's motives in the Nevaeh Hudson case."

"He did?" she said, practically yanking the phone out of his hand. Jason had been investigating her lead. Among the search results, there was a report from the local newspaper with a photograph of the psychiatrist taken just recently, and the caption underneath said, "*Renowned psychiatrist believes killer might be striking women at random.*"

She scoffed. "Bullshit."

"Exactly," Jason said as he stepped aside to let her go through the revolving door first. "So you're right. He could be our guy. Let's go check him out."

CHAPTER TWENTY ONE

Laura Porter's eyes snapped open when she heard a squeak next to her ear.

Rats.

She couldn't see them, but she could certainly hear them. They seemed to come from everywhere and anywhere, at once. Even *inside* her, as if they'd already gnawed into her brain.

The unsettling thought made her gasp. She sat up in a panic, but her hands were tied to a heating pipe behind her back. Though she'd experienced such a thing before, it all seemed so unreal to her, as if it were some horrible nightmare. Back then, they'd all told her that she'd been in the wrong place at the wrong time. That it was a once-in-a-lifetime tragedy. Surely, this kind of horrible thing didn't happen to people twice. This time, it *had* to be a nightmare.

But her hopes of suddenly waking up in her bed at home and snuggling under the covers dwindled with every minute she was stuck in this rat hole.

Happy endings weren't always guaranteed. She'd learned that the first time she'd been tied up.

And now, here she was again.

Laura shuddered. *I always thought I had the worst luck. Now, I know I do.*

With intense focus, she sifted through her memories. She remembered the groaning figure that had descended the ladder. A single black mass, its hulking strides bringing it ever closer. The mask, that horrible, ghastly Halloween mask with the fathomless red eyes and white, dead skin. Hands, poking and prodding at her. A voice that sounded inhuman, saying things, terrible things. *You want to die, don't you? Your life isn't worth anything. I am going to end that suffering for you, once and for all.*

And then … then … she couldn't remember.

He'd left her down here alone. But she knew he wouldn't stay gone for long. He'd come back.

Again.

They always came back.

She knew that better than anyone. Just when you thought things were bad, they could always get worse. He would come back to her, and then he would make everything worse.

She had no time to lose.

Pull yourself together. Think!

But the ungodly stench, and most of all, her hunger and the unbearable thirst, had left her weakened, clouded her senses. Laura's mouth was dry as parchment. She pushed out her tongue to reach for the drops that sporadically fell from the ceiling. Then she tried to loosen her bonds.

Don't be silly. You know that's not going to work.

Before, the rope had been so tight that it had cut off the blood flow to her hands. Laura had tried, over and over again, finally giving up when her wrists were chafed raw and the rope soaked with sweat and blood. She'd tried until all hope was gone and she was certain that she would die down here. She'd even tried to make peace with that fact, the fact that she'd soon see her family again.

But the thought of just how he might kill her sent a jolt of fear through her. As much as she wanted to see her family, as the moments ticked on and she was left to think endlessly about what kind of torture he might put her through, she realized she wasn't ready for that. Could one ever be ready for that?

So she could think of nothing else to do. No other way of escape.

Just try one more time, her husband's voice seemed to beg her.

All right, I will, she told him, feeling silly that she'd gotten so sick and delirious now that she was talking to a dead person.

Taking a deep breath, she slid her backside up against the pipe. Dizzy from the pain that pulsed through her wrists like electric shocks, she was about to fall into a stupor when suddenly a tiny bit of space opened up between her and the pipe.

Laura made another attempt. And another. And another. The space widened.

Laura clenched her teeth and stifled a scream as she violently jerked her hands out of the restraints. For several long seconds, darkness descended on her.

She stared at her hands in disbelief. *How did that work? Was it some kind of miracle?*

When she came back to herself, she looked up the ladder leading to the hatch. Well, she assumed it was a hatch. The ladder was too long, and it disappeared in darkness.

A last ember of strength flared up inside her, momentarily numbing the pain. She willed herself to stand, but she struggled to lift her feet, stumbling toward the ladder on almost completely numb legs.

Laura staggered across the room until she hit the wall of rough wooden slats and barbed wire. With her right hand, she grabbed the bottom rung. Blood trickled from her wrist and down to her elbow. When she tried to reach for the next rung with her other hand, she suddenly felt it: she had lost all control of her left arm, which hung limply at her side like a malfunctioning foreign object. No matter how hard she tried, her arm refused to obey.

With helpless eyes, she gazed up the ladder. Eventually, she grabbed on to it with one hand while her bare feet searched for a foothold in the cracks of the brittle wall to push herself up. Her muscles shook with the effort.

Then it happened. A couple of the rickety construction of boards and wire gave way and collapsed in on itself with a crash. Laura screamed as she slammed onto the ground, staring up at the broken boards.

Her scream echoed. She felt sure that at any moment, her captor would return, and he would not be happy. He'd glare at her with the mask's unfeeling eyes and tell her she was going to die.

But that did not happen. She waited a minute, two, but there was nothing but silence.

Then she looked up at her escape.

This time, as she stared up at the rustic ladder, the six remaining rungs she could see looked like an insurmountable obstacle. Like a mountain, impossible to climb. All her strength had gone.

She closed her eyes and thought about her children. Her loving husband, Phillip. How many nights had she cried herself to sleep, wishing she could be with them again?

But every time she did, she always heard her children's voices. *Not yet, Mommy. Not yet. You have more to do down there. We will see you soon.*

Now, she wondered if it was finally time.

She'd been through enough since the tragedy. She'd seen all three of those gang members sent to prison, given multiple life sentences which assured they'd never see the light of day. She'd spoken at the sentencing, ensuring that people would not soon forget the names of her family members who had perished. She had done her work for her family. Maybe this was the universe's way of saying she was finally ready.

But then she heard it, clear as day, again. *Not yet, Mommy. Not yet. You have more to do down there. We will see you soon.*

And when she opened her eyes, there was a bright light filling the room. It was so beautiful, it left her breathless.

Now she could see the top of the hatch, clear as day.

It was open. Incredibly, her door to escape was completely open, and without an obstacle in between.

All the pain seemed to drain from her body and a sudden burst of energy propelled her forward. She grabbed ahold of the wooden ladder, and this time, without any fear, she began to climb.

CHAPTER TWENTY TWO

Nora stood in front of an enormous stone mansion, on one of the nicest streets in the town of Carlton, only a mile from the campus of Carlton University. There was only one light on in the home, on the third floor.

"Hell, being a professor and knowing all the things about psychiatry must pay well," Jason said under his breath. "Who knew? I'm in the wrong line of work, Price."

"Oh, like you'd give up this glamour for anything," she said, wiping the cookie crumbs from his tie—remnants of his little snack at Elle Squires's apartment. "Let's go. Leave the talking to me."

"Yes, ma'am," he said with a mock salute as they climbed the imposing stone staircase with the giant lions on each railing.

She went up and, without hesitation, lifted the knocker on the heavy wooden door and let it fall three times.

A moment later, the door opened, and an older woman peered out. "Yes?"

She showed her badge. "Nora Price, and this is my partner, Jason Snyder, from the FBI. We're looking for Dr. Fitzsimmons."

"Oh dear," the woman said, covering her mouth. "Is there some trouble?"

"No, it's just an investigation we're conducting," Nora said, looking around the foyer. From her spot at the door, she could already tell the foyer was enormous, and as elegant and stuffy as its owner. "Are you his wife?"

"Housekeeper. Usually, when you want to consult on a case, you come at a normal hour," the woman pointed out, her eyes narrowing. "It's quite late and the doctor told me he didn't want to be—"

"It's all right, Bernice," a voice boomed from somewhere above.

Nora knew that voice. As Bernice looked behind her and reluctantly opened the door wider, Nora saw him—the esteemed man himself, standing on the balcony overlooking the foyer. Seeing him there, looming over them, she remembered how she'd dreaded every moment she'd spent in his presence.

She swallowed the bitter taste in her throat and stepped in. "Dr. Fitzsimmons, I'm—"

"I get it, I get it. You're someone with the bureau and you want to consult on the case. I heard all that, and to tell you the truth, I don't really care who you are," he said, striding down the long, curved staircase toward them. "Of course I'll comply, but I'm a busy man so I can't afford you much time. This way."

He reached the bottom of the staircase and glided toward the right, through an arched doorway. His movements were elegant as a dancer's, and his body was almost skeletally thin. That was another thing she remembered hating about him—adding in his colorless skin, he looked like a living corpse.

When they reached an elegant living room with a massive fireplace, Victorian furniture, and dark mahogany wainscoting, he spun on them without asking them to take a seat. "What do you need, and make it snappy. I'll give you one minute."

He held up a finger, almost touching her nose with it, and Nora recalled yet another thing she'd hated about him. His fingers were so bony, from the first knobby knuckle to the meticulously manicured fingernail. And the way he wagged his finger in her face, she felt like he was talking to his dog.

Taken aback, Nora looked over her shoulder to see Bernice, quietly closing the double doors to give them privacy. She said, "Yes, we're consulting about a case. It's the—"

"I'm sure it's the murders. Those women. Yes?"

"That's right," she said, surprised. "You've been consulted about them before?"

"Not by your bureau," he said, inspecting something on his fingernail, as if bored. "But the police have hounded me constantly on it, wanting me to help them get inside the killer's brain. As if they can't think a single thought for themselves. I told them what I'll tell you now. This killer is too sharp. You're going to have to be on the top of your game to catch him. And so far, I haven't seen anyone that seems up to the challenge. You two included."

Nora frowned. Now, she *really* remembered why he'd rubbed her the wrong way. That condescending little smirk of his. Never quite meeting her eyes. Treating her like she was just another number. "We think the killer might be someone you've worked with."

For the first time, he met her eyes. He blinked, and his face registered something new. Surprise. "Now, that *is* interesting. Why do you say that?"

"Because we believe all of the victims might have seen either you or one of the therapists that have been mentored by you."

He shook his head. "I haven't seen patients in years. I'm too busy." He reached into his pocket and pulled out a long chain. Attached to it was a pocket watch.

And with that, Nora forgot how to breathe.

As he looked casually at the face, she brought a hand to her heart to still it. Something about the watch, the chain, stirred up the strongest sense of déjà vu she'd ever had. She felt as though the walls were bending in on themselves, and the floor was waving like in a funhouse.

Dr. Fitzsimmons spoke, saying something about how he had to finish a paper, and how he had no more time to offer them, but his voice came out distorted and strange. Nora stood there, frozen, unable to speak. As he looked up, his face had just begun to register something—was it recognition?—when Jason spoke up.

"Uh, so you've seen the news reports. You've weighed in on some of them, too, we noticed. You didn't notice the connection to your own clientele?"

The doctor set the watch back in his pocket and barked out a laugh. Nora felt her heartbeat slow as he said, "Agent, I've worked with every therapist in this county. I daresay you could connect every one of their patients to me. So no, it didn't strike me."

He turned to look at Nora, whose face had lost all color. Suddenly, she felt small and sick, the way she'd been most of her life before becoming an agent. Like a victim.

"You're familiar," he said. "Why is that?"

"Because I was one of your last patients," she spat out, still staring at the pocket where he'd dropped that watch.

The man who took her and Sophia had to have been wearing one. Why else would it strike such terror in her heart? And this man had been living in Blackburn County for years, working with crimes. He'd never been caught. He'd waited, biding his time, before giving in to his diseased brain and striking out again.

"Ah," he said. "Sorry. But that was too long ago. I don't remember."

"You know criminal psychology inside and out. Tell me, Doctor," she said, her voice louder and stronger. "Do you believe that people who study crime, who make it their life's work, are more likely to commit it?"

"Of course not. It's most likely stemming from childhood abuse, or—" He stopped and stared at her. "What are you insinuating?"

"You've been speaking as the authority on all these murders, with intimate knowledge of them," she said, putting her hands on her hips. "And yet do you have an alibi for any of them?"

"What?" he blubbered, shocked. "This is preposterous! That I could—"

Jason said, gently, "Char, I don't know that—"

"It's him," she whispered under her breath. "The watch. I remember it. I remember it all. I know it's him."

Her partner's jaw dropped in shock. "Seriously?"

She stepped between the men and faced the man she'd always wanted to catch, to put away, to make suffer, and it gave her great pleasure to say, "Dr. Fitzsimmons, you are under arrest."

*

It was nearly midnight.

Nora sat in her cubicle at headquarters, staring at her computer screen. And yet all she saw, again and again, was that pocket watch.

She tried to see more. She strained with all her might to see past it, to see something other than a man, dangling that long chain with the silver watch on it. But she saw nothing.

Still, she was sure. She *had* to be right. The man was a creep, he'd hung around the crimes as if he were playing some sick cat-and-mouse game. He'd been enjoying this. Back then, with Sophia. And now, too. She gritted her teeth with disgust at the thought.

A moment later, Jason walked in, shirt sleeves rolled up, a cinnamon five o'clock shadow on his chin, and leaned against her desk. "You finish it?"

"Huh?" She looked up, confused.

"The report." His eyes went to the computer screen. Then he leaned in and pressed a button. The computer roared to life. "Helps if you actually turn it on."

She sulked, sinking deep into her chair. Then she looked up at him. "Do you think I was wrong?"

She hoped he'd say, immediately, that she was right on the button. But she knew he wouldn't lie. Instead, he shrugged and said, "You feel what you feel. I can't help you untangle those memories."

He couldn't. Which was why Durham had come down on her. She'd brought Dr. Fitzsimmons downtown, feeling so proud of herself, feeling like maybe she could actually say that she'd done right by her sister for once in her life.

But then she'd questioned Fitzsimmons, and it all went downhill. Not only did he deny kidnapping Laura Porter and Sophia, he denied it all. Then he'd told them he wanted his lawyer, that he would sue the pants off all of them, especially *her*, and promptly shut his mouth. So of course, she wasn't Durham's favorite person right now.

"I was just so sure," she said in a quiet voice. "But a stupid memory fragment is not going to hold up in court, is it?"

He squeezed her shoulder and then went to turn off the computer. "Come on. I'll take you home. You can write up the report in the morning."

She felt like she'd gone fifteen rounds in a heavyweight match. She didn't want to think about the case anymore. At that moment, she wanted nothing more than to climb into bed and sleep. "No, you go ahead. I want to finish this up."

"All right. Get some sleep, though, Price. You're a mess when you don't," he said, patting her head affectionately before heading out the door.

It was no use, though. Her mind was mush. She wound up staring at the computer screen for another fifteen minutes before deciding to call it a day. Grabbing her things, she walked toward the exit of the near-empty headquarters, head down, feet dragging.

Before she could make it there, though, Durham poked his head out of his office. "Price," he barked.

She turned, groaning. Hadn't her boss already chewed her out enough? Did he have to come back for round two?

"There's news," he said. "Laura Porter's been found."

CHAPTER TWENTY THREE

Nora couldn't keep her hands still. She piled them in her lap as they drove, and then, two seconds later, began to chew like a maniac on any free bit of fingernail she could find. "Can you go a little faster?" she asked the cab driver.

"Sure, if you want me to rear-end this ambulance," he said as they pulled into the front driveway of the hospital.

Before he could even come to a complete stop in the overhang in front of the entrance, she jumped out and ran inside.

She had to see Laura.

Laura Porter, who'd already survived the unthinkable, had been found in the eastern part of the county, walking along the highway. Like Miranda, she'd flagged down the driver of a passing car, who took her to safety. Word was that she'd been kidnapped and held in the basement of an abandoned cabin, much like Miranda had been.

But she was alive. And she had made it out of a traumatizing situation, not once, but twice. Nora wanted to be among the first to question her.

The hospital receptionist directed her to Laura's room in the ICU. When Nora arrived, she paused at the door, expecting to see a shaking, frightened shadow of a woman in that hospital bed. But when she stepped inside for her first look at the woman, she was surprised. The victim was sitting up in bed, eating what looked like some chocolate pudding.

She looked younger than someone who was pushing forty, with her hair pulled back into a ponytail, tendrils hanging down into her face. She was pretty, with darker skin and bright green eyes, and other than the bandage wrapped around her head, she looked just as unaffected as Miranda had been. *Numb,* Nora thought. *Too much trauma.*

"Laura," she said gently, showing her ID. "I'm Nora Price from the FBI. We've been looking for you."

Laura smirked. "Well, you found me. Or I guess you can say … I found you. I don't think you would've found me, where I was."

"And why's that?"

"It was in some broken cabin that was more like a hole in the ground, and it was way in the woods."

That sounded familiar. "How are you doing, under the circumstances?"

"Fine." She looked down at herself. "The police wanted to take pictures of my injuries. I haven't been photographed in ages. All the photos of my family were burned up in the fire, and I just never wanted to have a photo of myself taken, afterwards. Sometimes, I don't even want to look at myself."

That sounded as if it could've come right from Nora's own mouth. She was so weighed down by the guilt that she hated to look at herself, too, even just to fix her hair in the mirror.

"Do you remember anything about your captor?" she asked gently.

Laura nodded. "I remember too much about him, unfortunately. Not that it'll help you identify him. He was tall, probably six feet. Skinny. But I couldn't tell you what he looked like, because he wore a mask, with one of those voice-changing machines that made him sound like a robot."

Height and build jived with the man they currently had in custody, but Nora had to be sure. She pulled out her phone and found a picture of Dr. Fitzsimmons. "Could this be him?"

Laura shrugged. "I guess. It's hard to tell, considering I didn't see his face. Who is that guy, though? I don't know him."

"He knew one of your therapists." Nora put her phone in her pocket and dragged a chair closer. "When you didn't show up at work, your friend Tammy went to check on you and found you missing, with signs of a struggle and blood. She called the police, and that's why we were put on the case. Why don't you tell me what you remember about it?"

"Yeah, I didn't lock the door, and he must've gotten in that way. I don't really remember much." She touched the bandage at her temple. "He must've hit me over the head because I don't remember anything after that until I woke up in a basement."

Nora let out an uneasy breath. This sounded very familiar to Nora, but she wasn't sure if she'd heard it from Miranda, or if it echoed her own story. "And then what happened?"

"When I woke up, I was alone, tied to a pipe. I tried to get out, but the rope was too tight, so tight I could barely feel my hands. And then he came down this ladder and started poking at me with a knife, telling me I was worthless and going to die. I thought he was going to kill me, but he didn't. He just tightened the rope around my wrists and left. I must've passed out again, and then when I woke up, I was able to wiggle the ties free and escape."

Nora listened, her brow wrinkling in confusion. "He tightened the bonds, but when you woke up, they were loose? Did he come back while you were passed out, you think?"

"I don't know. I don't understand it either. It just keeps coming back to me in pieces." She cradled a hand against her head in frustration.

Nora knew that feeling well. "I understand. Just tell me what you remember."

"I just remember that horrible robotic voice, telling me I was going to die. And then him leaning in, working the ties, his long fingernails scraping at my wrists. The ties were so tight, I thought my arms would fall off. Look at this."

She presented the underside of her wrists to Nora, showing not only the raw welts around her wrists from where the ties had been, but several smaller scratches.

A sick feeling descended on Nora as she inspected those red marks. They were claw-like scratches, the kind she used to get during tussles with her sister, Sophia, when she was trying to grow out her nails to make a pretty manicure. "Are those from his long fingernails?"

Laura nodded, and instantly, Nora went back to earlier that evening, when Dr. Fitzsimmons had placed a finger in front of her face.

Her stomach roiled. Dr. Fitzsimmons's fingernails had been perfectly manicured, and very short.

In that instant, something else occurred to Nora, something big, something she'd stupidly overlooked. How could she have been that blind?

Nora let out a sympathetic sigh and said, "Laura … did you attend a session with someone named Elle Squires?"

"Elle Squires?" Laura blinked in surprise and nodded. "Yes, she was the one doing that trauma therapy out of her home. How did you know?"

"How did you meet her?"

She let out a little, self-deprecating laugh. "Oh, I remember. I was in the supermarket, buying food. I never go down the sugary cereal aisle because my kids always used to beg me for it, and I thought it was so bad for them. But this time, I did, and I saw the cereal my little Billy used to always ask for. I started to think about how I'd give it to him breakfast, lunch, and dinner if I could just have him back. There I was, crying in the middle of the supermarket, and she saw me."

"What did she say to you?"

"Well, she was very nice. She consoled me. I don't remember what she said, but I instantly felt better. I told her she could do that for a living, and she laughed and said that she did. She told me about her practice and her therapies, and said I could come to a meeting that night, to check it out."

"And did you?"

"Yes. Well, I didn't undergo the therapy. I went to a demonstration, but it seemed too good to be true, so I never went back." She studied Nora. "Does she have something to do with all this?"

Nora stood up and pushed the chair back into place. "I'm not sure. But I'm going to find out."

CHAPTER TWENTY FOUR

Nora knocked on the door of the apartment building penthouse a little after midnight.

Elle Squires took a while to come to the door, but she did come, peering out in spectacles, a confused look on her face. "Agent Price. I'm surprised to see you back here at this hour. Did you forget something?"

"I just had a few more questions for you," she said.

Elle didn't open the door more than a crack. "Well, it is late, and I'm still working on that report I mentioned for Dr. Fitzsimmons, so—"

"That's why I knew you'd still be awake," Nora said, putting her hand on the door. "Please. It'll only take a few minutes."

Finally, Elle opened the door to let her in. "Okay, if you're sure. But I really do—"

"Don't worry," Nora said, turning toward the therapist to be sure to gauge her reaction. "Dr. Fitzsimmons won't be waiting for it, seeing how he's in jail, about to be charged for the murders of Nevaeh Hudson and Joy Klasky, and the kidnappings of Miranda Forster and Laura Porter."

As expected, Elle's eyes widened. "What do you mean?"

"We have evidence that we believe will show he's responsible," she said, taking a seat on one of the cushions as Elle sunk next to her, staring in confusion. "But you can help us build our case. Is there anything you might have noticed with him? Anything off at all?"

Shell-shocked, she stared at her lap. "Well, I suppose he's always been a little odd. He talked incessantly about the murders. I just thought it was professional courtesy, but …" She pressed her lips together and brought a finger to touch her chin. "But yes, now that you do mention it, I think it could be him."

Nora stared at that finger. A long, polished fingernail.

Elle Squires was tall, too, easily approaching six feet, and very thin. With a mask, and a voice changer … yes.

"After all, you were sending your research to him, on all of your clients and the participants in your study, right …?" Nora went on. "That's where he must've gotten their information."

"Exactly," she breathed, shaking her head. "I can't believe it. I worked so closely with him. And he's so respected, with such a sterling reputation. I guess you never can know …"

Nora stared at the therapist, playing the part like a true actress. The woman didn't even realize how deep she'd stepped in it.

Until Nora snapped her fingers. "Wait. That can't be right. Laura Porter wasn't one of your participants. She was only an observer. And you never take down their information for the research, so you wouldn't have sent her name to Dr. Fitzsimmons."

Elle's eyes narrowed. "Oh. Well, I must've gotten her information some other way, then."

"Actually … none of them were actual participants. They were all just observers," Nora went on. "So none of them should've been sent to Dr. Fitzsimmons. Which makes me wonder if he is indeed our connection. In fact, it seems a better bet that Dr. Fitzsimmons is not our connection at all, but *you* are."

Nora waited for a response, but Elle said nothing. She simply looked around the room, as if looking for escape.

"I don't know why I didn't think of it before. Likely because all along, we've been looking for a man. But you could've done it all, too. You're tall, and under those delicate, flowing outfits, I bet you're quite strong. You could easily have disguised the female parts of your body the same way you disguised your face and voice," Nora continued.

Finally, Elle scoffed and stood up, smoothing out her long skirt. "This is ridiculous."

"Is it?" she demanded, to which Elle froze. "It all makes sense now. You getting in touch with me, saying that you were sure you'd seen Laura Porter before. You knew we would make the connection eventually, and you needed to cover your tracks. What did you say? 'They showed her photograph on the news. And it just clicked.' Isn't that right? No, you didn't. They couldn't have shown a photograph of her, because she herself said she hadn't had any taken, and just about all the rest had been destroyed in the fire. There's only one known photo of her, and it was on the fridge at her house—and no one but the authorities saw it."

"Stop it. You're embarrassing yourself," she said, tossing her hair and marching toward her desk. "You have no proof of anything you're saying, so please, leave me alone."

"Actually, I think we do. Your fingernails scratched Laura when you were tightening her bonds. Or were you loosening them, because you wanted her to be found, because you were scared that we were getting too close?" She tilted her head. "Anyway, apparently, you didn't wear gloves, and we've been able to collect DNA samples."

She stopped and swallowed, then crossed her arms. "So what are you going to do? Am I under arrest, then?"

Nora would have, but she'd used her only pair of cuffs on Dr. Fitzsimmons, and she was ill prepared to arrest two people in one night. "I'm going to call for the police and bring you in for questioning."

Remarkably calm, Elle Squires looked at her computer. "You mind if I finish this up, then, first?"

Nora reached for her phone and shrugged. It didn't matter anyway. All that mattered now was that she atoned for her recent flub by bringing in the right suspect. And this time, she knew she had it right.

As Elle typed away at her computer, she called headquarters and got Durham's voicemail. Then she called the receptionist. "Yeah, it's Agent Price. I need police down here immediately at the Elm Street Apartments."

"Address?"

She frowned. She didn't know that. "One second."

She was about to walk to the window and look out at the nearest street sign, but then she realized that the typing had stopped. She looked over at the chair near the laptop. It was empty, and Elle Squires was nowhere to be found.

"Excuse me, Agent?" the receptionist asked, as Nora's heart shook in her chest. She slowly dug a hand under her blazer to pull out her sidearm.

Before she could even touch it, though, she felt a rush of air, and something hard and heavy slammed into the back of her skull. Her surroundings went blurry, and then everything fell away.

CHAPTER TWENTY FIVE

Elle Squires hated people like this.

The know-it-alls. The ones who seemed to have all the answers.

Too many of those in the world, she thought as she looked at the body of the FBI agent, curled up on her living room floor.

It was her mission in life to rid the world of them. And if she couldn't do so with her treatments, she'd find another way.

Like this.

Agent Nora Price had been wrong to doubt her. Just like all the others. They'd looked at her like some kind of snake oil salesman. Just because she was trying to help? They'd dealt with trauma all their lives, and Elle had dedicated her life as a therapist to them. This was how they repaid her?

In her eyes, they deserved everything they got.

But this was going to pose a problem.

She drummed her fingers on the table as she looked at the agent's body, now wrapped in blankets. Stupid woman, coming here. Now she'd have to figure out how to get her out of the apartment unnoticed.

Still, she'd faced bigger, harder problems in her life. An abusive father, a mother who ignored her, a string of tragedies that had shaped her outlook on the world, cementing her desire to study trauma and its effects on the human brain. From her studies, she learned one, overarching thing: A person could let a tragedy either consume them, or transform them.

And she had. She'd once been so quiet, shy, and meek. Now, she was fearless.

And strong.

And everything she hadn't been before.

Luck was on her side. Due to the late hour, she saw no one as she dragged the body down the hallway to the elevator. No one as she reached the parking garage. No one as she loaded the agent's body into her trunk and sped out into the night.

From then on, as she headed toward the woods, she knew it would be smooth sailing. After all, she'd scouted dozens of locations for this kind of thing. Cabins in the woods that were either abandoned or used only sporadically by hunters. She knew these woods like the back of her hand, ever since her father had insisted on bringing her out here on his hunting trips. As much as she'd hated to kill animals, if she said no, she'd get a slap to the face, so she'd learned to live with it … and then she'd learned to love it.

Even now, she loved whenever anyone or anything was in peril. It made her giggle.

Try untangling that, Dr. Fitzsimmons, she thought. He'd always sought to understand his patients. But Elle had been so successful because she knew there was no understanding it. Which was what she whispered to her patients, every time, during the therapy.

Pretty thing. Worthless thing.

She just told them what they already believed. Somehow, accepting it made everything better.

When she pulled down the long, gravel driveway toward her final destination, a cabin that had partially been destroyed by fire and left to disintegrate into the ground, she smiled. Yes, acceptance was the key.

And long ago, she'd accepted just who she was: a monster.

CHAPTER TWENTY SIX

"Come on, Agent! Wake up, lazybones! Time's wasting!"

Nora started awake in absolute shock, sputtering as a bucket of cold water was dumped on top of her. She looked around and found herself on the floor of a windowless room, her wrists bound behind her, around a rusted old heating pipe.

In front of her was the sweet, happy therapist who'd led that life-changing, standing-room-only session she'd been at, only hours ago. After that, it got hazy, but from the pain on the side of her head, she must've knocked her out…

And now she was here. In the same place she'd been, she was sure, with Sophia, all those years ago. All the fear and uncertainty flooded back at once, and she shuddered. She wanted to scream Sophia's name, to find her …

But even though the memories were thick, she blinked them away. She had to stay in the present.

Elle Squires leaned in, looking closer at her. "Scared?" She smiled, then put a mask over her face. It was a ghastly face, with red eyes and pale skin. Her voice became robotic and emotionless. "How about now?"

No. Nora, this isn't the same person who kidnapped Sophia. It can't be.

Vomit gurgled in the back of her throat as she realized this woman was probably the last person to see Nevaeh Hudson and Joy Klasky alive. The thought of what she had done to them made Nora want to scream, but a wide strip of duct tape held her mouth shut.

Nora looked into some sort of chamber that lay half in ruins. The only furniture in the room was a camp table, with a number of rusted tools. She couldn't allow herself to think of what they might be used for. If she did, if she became too emotional, she'd never be able to escape.

Elle whipped the mask off, her long, curly hair crackling with static. "I guess I don't need this stupid thing. My cover's already blown with you. I never could breathe in it anyway," she said, casting it aside. "It doesn't really matter. You're soon going to be dead."

Nora eyed her, a chill running over her as she tried to focus her vision. Everything was blurry, either from the lack of light or the injury to the back of her head. She couldn't tell how bad it was, but she felt something crusted in her scalp, probably blood.

Elle looked over the assortment of tools. "The only question is, how to do it? I like to vary my method, to keep people like you guessing. I'd planned to use this on Miranda, but then she got away, the bitch. Then Laura … well, let me just tell you that I was not a happy camper."

She pulled out a long, thin scalpel, staring at it with adoration.

"Pretty, huh? But *you* ruined that one. You and your pretty-boy partner. I was so worried you were on my tail, I had to let her go. I thought I'd wait, bide my time. Maybe move somewhere else before I started my work again." As she spoke, her right eye started twitching nervously. And then, like magic, her sneer gave way to a wide-eyed, almost innocent expression. "And then you found me, and so I had no choice but to act!"

The twitch around her eye grew worse.

Elle moved over to the other side of the small room and pointed a spotlight and a video camera at Nora. Nora blinked in the light as she looked over each of the weapons there.

"Hope you don't mind if we record this," she said, flipping on the video camera so a red light blinked at Nora. "So, do you like it?" she said, her voice suddenly as dull as the rusted blades on the table.

Nora shrank back as she returned, waving the blade of the scalpel in front of her face.

"What do you think I'm going to do with this?"

Her eyes lit up with an almost fanatical fervor as she stroked the blade across Nora's cheek, its touch so soft, she could barely feel it.

"Yes, look at me, look at me! There's nothing like that glorious fear in your eyes! Such a pretty face—I hope you're not too attached to it."

A caught scream gurgled in Nora's throat. She pressed her back up against the radiator and looked desperately toward the door of the cabin, thinking of Jason. How desperately she wanted him to storm in and tackle this madwoman to the ground.

But she was in the middle of nowhere. He would never know what happened to her out here. It was likely no one would ever find her.

"Aw, honey," Elle said sympathetically, tracking her line of sight to the door. "You're on your own, I think. You probably don't remember it because you were down for the count, but we went somewhere very,

very far away this time. That handsome partner of yours can't save you now."

Nora stared, speechless, because she knew Elle was right. She was alone. Just as alone as she'd been on that day. She'd managed to escape that day by sheer dumb luck, and dumb luck rarely struck twice.

It shook Nora to the core. Beside herself, she jerked on the heating pipe, trying to free her hands from the restraints, to somehow peel the tape off her mouth. A pathetic and futile endeavor.

Elle Squires watched her, rapt and amused, as if she knew she had no hope. Any second now, she would decide Nora's fate.

Decide the way she was to die.

A disconcerting smile graced Elle's lips, a smile that was nothing at all like the smile of the friendly therapist with the soft cushions, flowy skirts, and colorful sandals.

"Don't you get your hopes up—nobody has ever left this basement alive. But don't worry, after all these years of fruitless investigations, I won't let you die in ignorance."

She sat down on a folding chair and looked at Nora.

"You know, Elle Squires is just a figment of my imagination. My name is Katie Fenway, and, oh, I'm also not a therapist, never was." She laughed, obviously pleased with herself. "My papers, the job references, my credentials—all of them fakes, which, by the way, nobody even seems to have really looked into. But who suspects the therapist? All they want is to decode people, don't they?"

Nora tried not to gag as Squires wistfully shook her head. "But not me. I've been through my own, you see. My father and mother used to leave me alone for most of my childhood. When my father came home, he'd beat me. Ah, but I don't cry about it, now. I certainly don't like to talk about it and ask for pity. Because I know the only way to move forward after trauma is to use it. To let it transform you. And it has."

She was staring Nora straight in the eye now. "It's made me strong. So strong, I can do anything."

A god complex. That's what this woman's trauma had given her. It had made her believe—falsely—that she had a right to decide who lived and who died.

"I know what you're thinking. That I think I'm better than everyone else. Some kind of god," she said with a small smile. "But a god wants power all to herself. And me? I wanted to share it. I *tried* to. That was what my sessions were all about."

Nora was breathing fitfully through her nose, half unnerved that this psychopath could understand her thoughts so intuitively, and half trying to make sense of the woman's confession. *Why the hell is she telling me all of this?*

Her eyes cold as ice, Squires looked at Nora. "But none of those other traumatized souls wanted my help. They laughed it off, decided never to come back. And why? Because they were weak. They wanted to learn to cope with their grief, talking it out, using medication … what's wrong with that picture?"

Nora's insides writhed, her vision blurring as she tried to spit out the many thoughts in her head. *You're crazy. You're insane. Listen to yourself!*

"It didn't matter how many people I helped with my therapy. I always looked at the ones I missed. The ones who didn't want my help. Who wanted to be wounded and pitied forever. And I decided that the world would be better off without them," she said, lifting the scalpel and holding it between them. She placed her finger at the very tip, and immediately, it started to bead with blood. "Just like you, right?"

Sweat trickled down Nora's temple, tickling the side of her face. She hoped it didn't look like she was crying. After her first ordeal, she'd spent a lot of time thinking about the way she would die. She didn't know when it would happen, or how, but there was one thing she knew above all else: She wanted to be strong in the end.

Please, God, let it be over.

Elle shook her head, holding the scalpel at the ready. "You laughed off my therapy. I saw you and your partner rolling your eyes, all smug, thinking you knew better. You *pathetic* person," she spat out. "You'd rather wallow in your self-pity forever, instead of taking control and finding real, meaningful change in your life. You're a therapist's worst nightmare. The person who keeps coming back, blaming everyone but themselves, and never, ever gets any better."

Nora swallowed, wishing her heart would stop beating so hard and loud. She yanked, one last time, sure that it would be as fruitless as the other times she'd tried. And of course, it was.

As Elle pranced around in front of her, swinging the scalpel, performing a show, Nora watched, thinking quickly. She breathed in through her nose, then out, her nostrils flaring.

"Don't worry, I know as well as you do how scary it is to face death, even a second time."

But Nora had been wrong about Miranda and Laura. She'd thought they'd become so used to the trauma, they were numb. Now, she knew it was something else.

It was courage. Pure, steel-coated courage.

So she wasn't scared in the least. This time, she stared at her captor, unblinking.

And when Elle Squires leaned in, taunting her with her weapon, Nora acted as easily as if breathing. In one, quick movement, she flung her head forward, smashing it into Nora's face. Rearing back, Squires inadvertently sent the scalpel scraping down her own neck. She let go of it, and it clattered to the floor.

Squires's eyes went wide, and she started to scream, rushing around the room, knocking over the table with all the sharp instruments. They fell with a clatter to the floor as she squealed in shock. Blood coursed down her white shirt. She grabbed a rag and held it to her neck, then a moment later, reached down on the ground. She'd found the blood-covered scalpel and wielded it with even more purpose now. "You are going to pay for this, you bitch! This is what I get for trying to help people!"

Stalking forward, she jabbed the weapon toward Nora.

"It's going to give me great pleasure to carve you up, you stupid woman."

Though the beating of Nora's heart drowned out all other noises, she soon became aware of the faint sound of barking from outside. Dragging her eyes wider, she listened.

She could've sworn she heard someone call her name, but she knew it was likely just wishful thinking. No one would find her out here.

It was just as that terrible thought began to settle in her brain that someone kicked in the door. Splintering into pieces, it fell from its hinges and clattered on the ground at her feet.

Nora blinked to focus on the figure silhouetted in the opening. It was Jason Snyder, his gun drawn.

"Hands up or I'll shoot!" he yelled.

But even wounded, Elle Squires wasn't ready to give up. "Put the gun down or your partner dies!" Squires countered.

Snyder placed his weapon on the ground. "All right, I did what you asked, now it's your turn! Drop the blade!"

But Elle Squires merely laughed. Her eyes gleamed with a fanatical light. "Nobody's going to interfere with my work, including you!"

In a flash, she rounded on Nora, just as Snyder went for his gun.

Mouth and arms bound, Nora moaned out in alarm, watching in utter shock as Elle lunged at her, the scalpel poised to slice her carotid artery.

Then a gunshot ricocheted through the small room.

Hand hovering inches from Nora's neck, Elle Squires froze, then sank to the ground.

Nora's heart was still hammering as Jason rushed toward her. Now there were other law enforcement in the room, too.

"Nora? Nora, listen to me," she heard someone say. It sounded like Jason, but it was muffled, as if he were speaking into a thick wool scarf. Then, louder: "Hurry, she needs help!"

Before her eyes closed, the last thing Nora saw was the paramedics rushing toward her, concern in their eyes. She felt the comforting sensation of someone wrapping a blanket around her shoulders and let out a long, relieved sigh. Then, dreaming of climbing into bed and taking a well-deserved rest, she drifted off.

CHAPTER TWENTY SEVEN

Nora woke to bright whiteness dancing beyond her eyelids, and thought she might be dead.

But then she smelled the acrid scent of disinfectant and heard the harsh beeping of the machines next to her. If this was paradise, she decided, those things wouldn't exist.

Her eyes fluttered open and slowly focused on a spare, white-walled hospital room.

This was familiar, too.

After the incident when she was a teenager, she'd woken up in a bed much like this one, surrounded by family and police officers, all eager to get her story. As she looked at the worried faces of her parents, she swallowed a bitter, prickly taste in the back of her throat. They looked expectant. *They want to know about Sophia. They want me to provide the detective with the information that will help find her. And I have to tell them I failed her, because I don't, can't remember ...*

But then she looked at the face of the detective and realized he wasn't one. It was Jason Snyder, her partner in the FBI.

The incident had happened years ago.

And they were not here for Sophia. They were here for her.

She blinked some more and tried to sit up, but her father stopped her and helped fluff her pillows. "Easy, Nora girl. You've been worrying us."

Her focus grew, despite the throbbing pain in her head. Because her right arm was tethered by an IV tube, she gingerly reached her left hand back there, finding a thick bandage. "How long have I been out?"

"Most of a day," her mom said, patting her shoulder.

She looked at her parents. They were mostly indoor people, never traveling very far, so whenever she came to their house for her Sunday dinner or lunch, they were usually dressed down. But they'd both put in the effort to look dressed up, which she knew was hard for them. Her mother was even wearing make-up. "Thanks for coming."

"Of course, you're our daughter," her father said, kissing the top of her head. "And we were so happy to hear that the doctor said you're going to be just fine."

"I know I am. I don't even know why I'm here. It was nothing, just a little bump on the head," she said, looking in disdain at all the wires attached to her.

Jason Snyder rolled his eyes. "Maybe because you were unconscious?"

"Asleep. I was just asleep! I was tired," she said, looking with worry at her parents. They always hated that she was an FBI agent, because they thought the danger involved brought them all the closer to losing another daughter. She said to them, "Really, it was nothing."

Jason must've gotten her drift, because he said, "Yeah. Just a fluke thing."

Mr. Price gave him a soft punch on the shoulder. "As her partner, you need to take care of her. Make sure nothing happens to her. I'm counting on you."

"Dad," Nora muttered warningly under her breath. He sounded like the father of a teenage girl, warning her first date to keep his hands to himself and have her home before curfew. Probably because he'd been robbed of the opportunity to do that for either of his daughters when they *were* teens. "I don't need anyone to babysit me."

"All right, all right," he said, holding his hands up in surrender. There was an awkward silence, wherein they all ended up staring at one another, until he nudged his wife. "Come on, dear. Let's leave these two to talk business."

"Oh, yes, I guess we should," she said, squeezing Nora's foot. "I'm glad you're on the mend. Call me."

"I will. Thanks for coming, guys," she said to them. They said their goodbyes, and the moment her parents were out the door, she looked at her partner. "What I didn't tell them was that I guess I actually did need someone to babysit me the other night. I'd probably be dead if it weren't for you. How did you find me?"

He shrugged as if it were nothing. "Squires must've forgotten to ditch your cellphone until much later, because we pinged it and found it about a quarter-mile from the cabin. As luck would have it, the cabin was on a list of abandoned cabins that the FBI had been compiling in the area. From there we tracked you, and the rest is history."

"I'm glad you did. I mean, weren't you heading off to sleep when I left you?"

He chuckled. "Couldn't sleep. Then I called in and found out Laura was alive, and went to the hospital, but you'd already gone. I talked to Laura and asked her to tell me what you two had talked about. It wasn't hard to put two and two together, since she said you seemed pretty hung up about Elle Squires. And then I realized that it made sense—we were looking everywhere but right at her. She had us all fooled, with that overly calm, sweet act she had going on."

"You can say that again," Nora said, shaking her head. "I'm just glad that Laura was able to escape. Apparently, Elle was afraid we were getting too close and wanted to throw us off her scent. What happened to her?"

"The wound was fatal," he said with a frown. "I just don't get how a respected therapist could want to do something like that …"

"That's the thing! She wasn't even an actual therapist. Apparently, she had her own trauma, and she thought she'd found the perfect way to deal with it. But the thing is, what works for one person won't work for everyone. In her twisted mind, she thought that everyone should be enthusiastic about her so-called methods. When someone wasn't, or questioned it, her mind rebelled. She took the rejection of her methods personally, as if those women didn't want her help, and wanted to wallow in their misery and grief forever," Nora said. Halfway through her rambling, she noticed that her partner's eyes had squinted in confusion, before glazing over entirely. Sometimes, explaining a madman's train of thought was impossible. "Or something like that."

He shrugged. "Well, whatever. We released Fitzsimmons, who by the way, isn't happy."

She winced. "He's going to sue, isn't he?"

"Apparently Durham was able to smooth things over with him," he said with a shrug, sitting on the edge of her bed. "It helped that he's supposed to be some big authority on the psychology of criminal masterminds and yet he didn't notice his own mentee, whom he apparently worked very closely with, was a psychopathic serial killer. I think he wants to just shove the whole thing under the rug."

She smiled. "Yeah, so much for his *the killer's selecting victims entirely at random* theory, huh?"

"Yeah. I read over some of his statements and apparently, he was wrong on all accounts. So I think he thinks it's probably better to just quietly walk away from it," Snyder said. "So, really, how are you? *Really*. Not some of that watered-down bullshit you feed to your parents to make them think you sit around working behind a computer all day."

"Fine. Just a little headache."

His eyes went to the ceiling. "You know I didn't mean that—"

"I know what you meant," she said, her voice rising. The machine next to her began to beep faster. She took a breath, willing her vitals to calm down, and said, "And no, being in that situation didn't bring any of the memories back. I mean, it felt familiar, and it was scary as hell, yes … but that's about it."

He pressed his lips together. She sensed disappointment, as if he wanted her to have closure almost as much as she did.

"But that's okay. You know what this experience made me realize?"

He leaned in, interested.

"I've tried a lot of different things, trying to work through it all on my own. But you know what I haven't tried? Group therapy. Not the kind Elle Squires champions, but an actual group of people who have gone through similar things." She smiled. "I realized that while talking to Miranda and Laura. I felt like people like them could understand me most. And so I want to give it a try."

He nodded. "Makes sense."

"Where's the call button?" she asked, looking around for it.

"Whoa. Not now!" he ordered, jumping off the bed. "Right now, you have to rest."

"I know. I just wanted another blanket. It's cold in here," she said, mostly to appease her partner. He was right—she needed to rest. She'd be out soon enough.

But he also knew how impetuous she was, and how much she wished she could speed up time. For the first time, when she thought about the future, there was a little excitement bubbling there. One might even call it hope. She couldn't wait to start.

*

"I'd like to give a special hello to the new attendees to our group," the leader, a small, white-haired woman named Cora said, smiling at each of the people in the circle. "Welcome to Wendy's Hope."

Several of the members of the group smiled, and Nora nodded. "Thank you."

It was a week since she and Jason had put to bed the Elle Squires case. When she was released from the hospital, Nora's search began in earnest. She was able to find a group in the neighboring town of Mendham, held in a church basement every Sunday evening. Apparently, the group was named after a local woman who was a survivor of a tragic event—a mugging on the streets of Boston in which the thief had not only murdered her fiancé, but shot her in the head, leaving her paralyzed from the waist down. When Nora had read about it, she felt an immediate solidarity with the brave woman, just as she had with Miranda and Laura. She knew, almost instantly, that she had to attend.

"Now, you don't have to speak. You're welcome to just listen," the woman said. "Like I said, I'm Cora, and I'm a social worker with the state. Who would like to start?"

Everyone seemed to be waiting for anyone else to say something. Finally, an older woman spoke up and told them all how she had fared over the last few days. Her voice sounded composed, though her eyes told a different story. The things she described seemed all too familiar to Nora.

Once she was finished, Nora said, "I would like to speak."

Nora was wearing a long skirt and high-collared silk blouse, and yet she could not remember ever having felt so naked. All eyes were on her.

"I'm Nora. I'm thirty-two… and my sister and I were victims of a kidnapping when I was a teenager," she said, slightly surprised at herself for having been able to get the words out. She tried to focus on what she was saying. "I am here today because I have decided I will no longer blame myself for what happened to my sister."

"That was great, Nora. You made the right call coming here. You're on your way now," the social worker said with a smile.

Nora was more than relieved when an overweight man in a bus driver's uniform raised his hand next, and all eyes shifted to him, instead. She felt the tension drain from her with every one of his words. After a while, she managed to look around and noticed a man who was vaguely familiar. But the déjà vu she experienced now was of a far different sort than she was used to.

It was actually pleasant.

After a moment, she realized why. He was the friendly man she'd seen at the session at Elle Squires's place. The man with the warm brown eyes.

Curious as to what had brought him here, she wished he'd speak, but he never did. But he'd been at the other session, too, which meant that like her, he was searching for answers. He did look at her and smile, which made her heart flutter a little. It was so rare to find a kindred spirit, especially considering her unique background.

After ninety minutes, the social worker brought the meeting to a close. She slapped her palms on her thighs and sent the people on their way with a few words of encouragement, intended to give them the strength they needed to make it through the week. And even though

Nora was still a bit uneasy, she left the church basement feeling reasonably well.

"Nora," a voice called after her as she climbed the steps.

She spun to find the man chasing after her, smiling. "Hey. I remember you," she said, fumbling to remember his name. "Uh …"

"Dane," he said with a grin, extending his hand to shake. "And you're Nora. That took a lot of courage for you to speak up like that. Your first time, huh?"

She nodded, surprised that the word *creep* hadn't even occurred to her until now. Because he didn't give off that vibe. Not at all. He seemed so … normal. "Yours?"

"My second. I still haven't worked up the nerve." He shrugged. "Maybe next week. Will you be here?"

She surprised herself by saying immediately, "Yes. I think it was good just to get it out, among people who understand. You should definitely try it next week."

"Maybe if you give me a nudge, I will," he said with a wink, and she laughed. There was a beat of awkward silence, and just when she was about to tell him she'd see him next week, he spoke up. "Hey, you wouldn't want to, I don't know—grab a cup of coffee sometime?"

She blinked. Dating had been off the table for so long. She'd had her share of relationships in high school and college, after the incident, but though some of them had lasted several months, none had staying power. Eventually, she'd decided that the burden inside her wasn't conducive to a relationship, because she knew she'd feel the weight of it even more if she forced someone else to share it with her.

But Dane was different. Here was someone who had his own burden. Maybe they'd be able to shoulder them together?

Then she realized she was getting ahead of herself. It was just coffee. Even if it led to nothing else, it would be great to have a friend who understood.

"Sure," she said with a smile. "Give me your phone and I'll put in my number."

"Great." He handed her his phone and she keyed the digits in.

They said their goodbyes and she headed out into the humid late summer night, her smile widening when only a moment later, she received a text from him: *Here's my nudge to you. How about this Thursday?*

EPILOGUE

Nora leaned back in her office chair and smiled at the text she'd received from Dane. *It's a date.*

Maybe it was.

She'd just confirmed the details of their coffee date, and she was surprised at how excited it made her feel. Excited, and nervous. She wasn't one to date much. But now she found herself doing a mental inventory of her closet, wondering what she should wear.

I have that brown dress with the flowers ... too dressy? Maybe I should keep it simple. Jeans and a T-shirt? Or ...

"What the hell is up with you?" Jason said, waltzing into her cubicle and sitting on the desk, as he often did. He was holding an *I live for Fridays* mug of coffee in his hands, and looked as if he'd stayed up all night.

"I could ask the same of you," she said, giving him the side-eye. "You kind of smell like a brewery. Did you even shower before you came in this morning?"

He scratched the cinnamon stubble on his chin. "Didn't have time. I had company, and she would *not* get out of my bed. What could I do? I wasn't going to kick her to the curb."

"You're *such* a gentleman," she teased, rolling her eyes just as her desk phone rang. She grabbed it and listened. It was the receptionist, telling her she had a guest out front. "Who?"

"Miranda Forster."

"Oh. Okay. Send her back."

She placed the phone back in the cradle and stood up, smoothing out the front of her slacks.

"Important date?" Snyder asked, eyebrows raised.

"Miranda. She's here to see me."

"You? Why you?"

Nora shrugged.

"Not me?" He seemed hurt.

Nora shrugged again and faced the doorway.

He sighed. "Well, I know where I'm not wanted. Give me a ring if you want to catch lunch," he said, stepping through her cubicle opening and disappearing into the sea of gray walls.

A moment later, Miranda appeared in her cubicle. She looked much healthier than she had in the hospital, a blush in her cheeks and a full face of make-up. She was holding a small package in her hands. "Agent Price," she said with a smile.

"Hi, Miranda," she said, giving her a small hug. "You look much better."

"I am better. I came by because my whole family wanted to thank you for everything you did to catch the person who kidnapped me." She handed her the gift. "This is just a small token of our appreciation."

"You didn't need to," Nora said, taking off the lid and pushing aside the tissue paper. At first, all she saw was gold. But then she realized it was in the shape of a bean. There was a wooden base, with a plaque that said, *Awarded to Nora Price, FBI Agent,* and the date. A little confused, she held it up. "Oh. It's lovely."

"It's the Golden Bean," Miranda said, rolling her eyes. "In the history of Forster's Beans, it's only been given out to thirteen people who have helped the family. You're one of them."

"Oh, really?" She patted her chest. "How thoughtful."

As she set it in a place of prominence on her desk shelf, knowing Jason would probably never stop making off-handed jokes about it, Miranda said, "I wanted to deliver it in person because I heard about you."

Nora looked back at her in confusion. "You did?"

She nodded. "What you went through. And I think it's really brave of you to have become an FBI agent after that. Most anyone would be so broken from it that they'd want to run away from danger. I know I did."

Nora frowned. She didn't feel like anyone's hero. In fact, it was precisely because she was so broken from the incident that she couldn't live a normal life, that she had to put herself through this. "Well, the past has definitely shaped me."

"It's inspired me. That something so good can come from something terrible." She wiped at the tears that came to her eyes. "Before this, I thought I'd never go to college. But now I'm applying to schools, and I want to major in criminal justice. I feel like you gave me hope. I can be strong, too."

"That's wonderful, Miranda," Nora said, putting a hand on her shoulder. "You'll be great at it, I'm sure."

Miranda's grateful face darkened then, and she said, "There is something else I wanted to tell you."

Nora raised an eyebrow.

Miranda lowered her voice and said, "The reason I knew about what happened to you is because my father's best friend was the lead investigator in the case."

Nora blinked. "You mean David Waldrup?"

"That's right. He was also the lead investigator when my father's first wife killed my half-brother," she said, matter-of-factly.

"He passed away, though," Nora said, recalling the article she'd read years ago. It must've been almost a decade by now.

"That's right. But he and my father used to talk about certain cases," she said, her brow wrinkling. "And I know I was very young, only about seven or eight, but I remember him talking about the captain of the police. I don't remember his name, but apparently, he was a dirty cop, involved in a drug operation, I think. And because of that, he did a lot of things to cover up his involvement, including destroying or concealing evidence of major crimes in Blackburn County. Waldrup said that even after he'd been put away, they were still uncovering evidence from those crimes, years later. He said there was so much evidence, it was just piling up in a big mess in a corner of the room. I remember him saying that some of the crimes, if they'd had the evidence at the time, would've been solved. But the police were trying to save face, so they never admitted to that."

Miranda was getting worked up, so Nora put a hand on her arm. After all the digging Nora had done into the case, she knew better than to get too excited about a new lead, since none of them ever panned out. "Okay, that's concerning. I know that there aren't many major crimes in Blackburn, but you still don't know that there was evidence concealed regarding *my* case. And without that knowledge, I can't very well—"

"I'm pretty sure he mentioned something about a kidnapping case. I know he talked about two sisters. And that he thought things would've been very different if they'd catalogued the evidence properly."

That made Nora stop and take notice. Her heart did a little flip. Of course, the first thing she'd done as an FBI agent was visit the police department's evidence room and check into the files on the case. The room had been a bit of a mess, but everything she'd found in regards to case #2347, she'd found to be all in order. Thin and unhelpful, yes, but in order.

But what if there had been more, and it wasn't filed properly? What if Miranda was right?

"You overheard that conversation years ago. There's no saying that evidence would still be there," she said quietly.

Miranda shrugged. "But it could be."

A possibility. Before, she'd been casually digging around and asking questions, never believing she'd find answers. She'd lived much of her life listening to those naysayers who told her Sophia was gone forever, pushing her under the near certainty that she'd never see Sophia again. That she'd never know the truth about what had happened to her older sister.

But this slim hope was enough to light a fire under Nora Price.

"I'll look into it," she promised, and she never broke one of those.

This, she felt, was a sign. A sign to do more. Not only that, it felt like the start of something. No, she wouldn't be moving on, like her parents wanted, because that wasn't possible.

This felt even better. It felt right.

NOW AVAILABLE!

CAN'T HIDE
(A Nora Price FBI Suspense Thriller—Book Two)

FBI Special Agent Nora Price is haunted by the childhood memory of being abducted, with her sister, by a notorious serial killer—and escaping, while her sister was never found. Now, a series of gruesome crimes leaves the community in fear as victims are discovered suspended upside down in trees, resembling chrysalises undergoing a horrifying transformation. In every case, Nora can't help but search for parallels to her own, determined to see if it's the same killer—and if her sister is still out there....

"This is an excellent book… When you start reading, be sure you don't have to wake up early!"
—Reader review for The Killing Game

CAN'T HIDE is book #2 in a new series by #1 bestselling mystery and suspense author Kate Bold, whose bestseller NOT ME (a free download) has received over 1,500 five star ratings and reviews.

A page-turning and harrowing crime thriller featuring a brilliant and tortured FBI agent, the NORA PRICE series is a riveting mystery, packed with non-stop action, suspense, twists and turns, revelations, and driven by a breakneck pace that will keep you flipping pages late into the night. Fans of Rachel Caine, Teresa Driscoll, and Robert Dugoni are sure to fall in love.

Future books in the series are now available.

"This book moved very fast and every page was exciting. Plenty of dialogue, you absolutely love the characters, and you were rooting for the good guy throughout the whole story… I look forward to reading the next in the series."
—Reader review for The Killing Game

“Kate did an amazing job on this book and I was hooked from the first chapter!”
—Reader review for The Killing Game

“I really enjoyed this book. The characters were authentic, and I see the bad guys as something we hear about daily on the news... Looking forward to book 2.”
—Reader review for The Killing Game

“This was a really good book. The main characters were real, flawed and human. The story went along quickly and wasn't mired in too many unnecessary details. I really enjoyed it.”
—Reader review for The Killing Game

“Alexa Chase is headstrong, impatient, but most of all brave with a capital B. She never, repeat never, backs down until the bad guys are put where they belong. Clearly five stars!”
—Reader review for The Killing Game

“Captivating and riveting serial murder with a twist of the macabre… Very well done.”
—Reader review for The Killing Game

“WOW what a great read! Talk about a diabolical killer! Really enjoyed this book. Looking forward to reading others by this author as well.”
—Reader review for The Killing Game

“Page turner for sure. Great characters and relationships. I got into the middle of this story and couldn’t put it down. Looking forward to more from Kate Bold.”
—Reader review for The Killing Game

“Hard to put down. It has an excellent plot and has the right amount of suspense. I really enjoyed this book.”
—Reader review for The Killing Game

“Extremely well written, and well worth buying and reading. I can't wait to read book two!”
—Reader review for The Killing Game

Kate Bold

Bestselling author Kate Bold is author of the ALEXA CHASE SUSPENSE THRILLER series, comprising six books (and counting); the ASHLEY HOPE SUSPENSE THRILLER series, comprising six books (and counting); the CAMILLE GRACE FBI SUSPENSE THRILLER series, comprising eight books (and counting); the HARLEY COLE FBI SUSPENSE THRILLER series, comprising eleven books (and counting); the KAYLIE BROOKS PSYCHOLOGICAL SUSPENSE THRILLER series, comprising five books (and counting); the EVE HOPE FBI SUSPENSE THRILLER series, comprising seven books (and counting); the DYLAN FIRST FBI SUSPENSE THRILLER series, comprising five books (and counting); the LAUREN LAMB FBI SUSPENSE THRILLER series, comprising five books (and counting); and the KELSEY HAWK MYSTERY series, comprising five books (and counting).

An avid reader and lifelong fan of the mystery and thriller genres, Kate loves to hear from you, so please feel free to visit www.kateboldauthor.com to learn more and stay in touch.

BOOKS BY KATE BOLD

KELSEY HAWK MYSTERY
DEAD INSIDE (Book #1)
DEAD RECKONING (Book #2)
DEAD TO ME (Book #3)
DEAD SILENCE (Book #4)
DEAD TO DAWN (Book #5)

ALEXA CHASE SUSPENSE THRILLER
THE KILLING GAME (Book #1)
THE KILLING TIDE (Book #2)
THE KILLING HOUR (Book #3)
THE KILLING POINT (Book #4)
THE KILLING FOG (Book #5)
THE KILLING PLACE (Book #6)

ASHLEY HOPE SUSPENSE THRILLER
LET ME GO (Book #1)
LET ME OUT (Book #2)
LET ME LIVE (Book #3)
LET ME BREATHE (Book #4)
LET ME FORGET (Book #5)
LET ME ESCAPE (Book #6)

CAMILLE GRACE FBI SUSPENSE THRILLER
NOT ME (Book #1)
NOT NOW (Book #2)
NOT WELL (Book #3)
NOT HER (Book #4)
NOT NORMAL (Book #5)
NOT AGAIN (Book #6)
NOT SAFE (Book #7)
NOT TODAY (Book #8)

HARLEY COLE FBI SUSPENSE THRILLER
NOWHERE SAFE (Book #1)
NOWHERE LEFT (Book #2)
NOWHERE TO RUN (Book #3)
NOWHERE LIKE THIS (Book #4)
NOWHERE GIRL (Book #5)
NOWHERE TO HIDE (Book #6)
NOWHERE CERTAIN (Book #7)
NOWHERE PURE (Book #8)
NOWHERE SOUND (Book #9)
NOWHERE SANE (Book #10)
NOWHERE TRUE (Book #11)

KAYLIE BROOKS PYSCHOLOGICAL SUSPENSE THRILLER
LAST BREATH (Book #1)
LAST CHANCE (Book #2)
LAST WISH (Book #3)
LAST SHOT (Book #4)
LAST MISTAKE (Book #5)

EVE HOPE FBI SUSPENSE THRILLER
IN HIS BLOOD (Book #1)
IN HIS SIGHTS (Book #2)
IN HIS REACH (Book #3)
IN HIS MIND (Book #4)
IN HIS WAY (Book #5)
IN HIS THOUGHTS (Book #6)
IN HIS DREAMS (Book #7)

DYLAN FIRST FBI SUSPENSE THRILLER
OUT OF REACH (Book #1)
OUT OF TOUCH (Book #2)
OUT OF TIME (Book #3)
OUT OF BOUNDS (Book #4)
OUT OF LUCK (Book #5)

LAUREN LAMB FBI SUSPENSE THRILLER
SOMETHING KNOCKING (Book #1)
SOMETHING CALLING (Book #2)
SOMETHING WRONG (Book 3)

SOMETHING DARK (Book #4)
SOMETHING TO HIDE (Book #5)

Made in United States
North Haven, CT
27 September 2025

80163137R00085